THE
NIGHT
CHILDREN

THE NIGHT CHILDREN

KIT REED

A TOM DOHERTY ASSOCIATES BOOK
NEW YORK

THE NIGHT CHILDREN

A Starscape Book
Published by Tom Doherty Associates, LLC
175 Fifth Avenue
New York, NY 10010

www.tor-forge.com

ISBN-13: 978-0-7653-2038-4
ISBN-10: 0 7653 2038 X

First Edition: October 2008

Printed in the United States of America

0 9 8 7 6 5 4 3 2 1

This book is for Cooper Reed, Jack Maruyama, Miranda Reed and Reed Elizabeth Maruyama, with love from their K.

THE
NIGHT
CHILDREN

ONE

WHEN YOU WALK INTO the mall you expect to come out at the end of the day.

You expect to come out, at least, but it's midnight and Jule Devereaux is locked in a car at the top of the gorgeous WhirlyFunRide, high above the sprawling Castertown MegaMall. She can pound on her glassy capsule and howl at top volume, and nobody will hear. Jule is used to getting what she wants, and what she wants more than anything right now is to get out, but she's trapped.

It is past midnight. The last shopper left hours ago.

She's alone in the biggest mall in the world.

The capsule Jule is riding in is stalled at the top of the great Ferris wheel, the highest point on the astonishing WhirlyFunRide. The world-famous ride is the crown jewel in the amusement plaza of the gigantic MegaMall.

Ordinary people from all over the world save up all their lives to come to the gleaming expanse of galleries and courtyards and domes that lights up the prairie outside Castertown. They'll borrow money or sell their houses if they have to, so they can afford to land near the airport hotel and spend a week shopping at the MegaMall. They're willing to stand in line for hours, just to take this ride.

Now, rich people can come to the MegaMall whenever they feel like it and spend as much as they want— sheiks, maharajahs, billionaires— but there's one thing everybody has to do. Even presidents and kings stand in line for the WhirlyFunRide.

Tonight plain old Jule Devereaux from Castertown Junior High has it all to herself.

She should have heeded the LAST CALL, but Jule has always been hardheaded. Now the glassy car she is riding in sways in place. It stopped for the night *this close* to the dome.

The monumental WhirlyFunRide is the glowing heart of the MegaMall, but it is her prison now.

Two hours ago there were gazillion shoppers swirling in the maze of marble corridors; there were thousands eating in the countless food courts of the MegaMall, but the place is still and empty now. Except for work lights twinkling far, far below, even the amusement plaza is dark.

Nobody knows Jule is here. She lost her cell phone, which is why she and Aunt Christy had the fight. Worse yet, there's nobody left at home that she can call. Where most kids have mothers and fathers, Jule lives with her aunt, and now Aunt Christy is gone.

Oh, she used to have a mother and father just like everybody else, but she lost them. Unless somebody came and took them away. Ten years later, she still doesn't know what happened to them. One night when she was very small she heard shouting outside. People slamming car doors. She has no idea what happened next. When she came downstairs next morning Aunt Christy was at the kitchen table, trying to pretend she wasn't crying. Mom and Dad were gone.

Now Aunt Christy is gone. They had a big fight last Sunday. When she came downstairs Monday morning the house was dead empty. It scared her sick.

She didn't even leave a note.

Jule could have phoned the police. She started to, but given what happened after her parents vanished, she hung up before the phone began to ring.

She's seen what happens to kids with nobody to take care of them. The Town Council sends them to the State Home. They would have taken her, if Aunt Christy hadn't promised to take care of her. The Town Council doesn't want anything to go wrong in Castertown, and they're quick to scoop up complainers and people who don't belong. With mighty Zozzco running the Town Council, everything in Castertown runs very smoothly. Thanks to Zozzco, the mayor keeps reminding them, everybody's happy and nobody's poor. If the police find out Jule is alone, they'll send the black car for her. There is no place in Castertown for orphans, which is what Jule is.

Or thinks she is. She doesn't know.

It still hurts to think about. What happened to them, anyway? Where is Aunt Christy now? Did she go out looking for them or was she taken? Jule doesn't know.

She made it through the first couple of days alone OK, but school's out, so she hasn't talked to anybody since Sunday night. Today the silence and loneliness got to her and she came to the mall. Just walking in her favorite entrance made her feel better, even though she doesn't have much to spend. She came in humming the Zozzco jingle kids in Castertown grow up on: "Spring and summer, winter, fall, cool kids shop at the MegaMall." She's been out here so many times that the MegaMall is like home to her, and the WhirlyFunRide?

It's better than home.

The combination thrill ride, roller coaster and gigantic Ferris wheel sends glossy cars rushing so high that they zip down the water chute at tremendous speeds. Then the sleek glass capsules hurtle around curves and up steep rises and more!

There are so many curves and loops in the Whirly-FunRide that you can't tell whether you're up or down. Near the end of the ride your car clicks into a slot on the enormous Ferris wheel and you ride up and up, into the beautiful glass dome at the exact center of the amusement park, the crown of the MegaMall. When your car reaches the top you're so high that you can see over the sprawling corridors and courtyards, all the way to the city of Caster-town.

Keep riding, girl. You might even see your parents from here.

It's weird, how a place can be so good to be in, and so bad for you.

Before Zozzco came, the whole town was poor. Nobody knows exactly what happened but people say that certain promises were made. The Zozzco Corporation and the Town Council of Castertown struck a deal. Money began pouring in. Suddenly everybody had a job! The glistening shoppers' paradise blossomed in the prairie like a gigantic flower.

Now the town is rich. The Castertown MegaMall and surrounding parks cover four square miles, and that's not counting the monorail or the international airport where bedazzled shoppers fly in every day just to cruise the galleries and shop the stores where they can find anything they want and everything's always on sale.

Nobody knows exactly how big the MegaMall really is. It's laid out like a gigantic honeycomb, except the bees aren't finished yet. Its boundaries grow and grow.

There are mall maps, of course, and store directories— at least for the sector where you happen to be wandering— but you can't begin to guess how many sectors there are, or what's going on in the parts you aren't allowed to see.

We're afraid to ask. Our town is riding high and the mall is magnificent, aren't we doing well?

Jule Devereaux is a lucky girl. When Zozzco gave Aunt Christy a job, Jule got her own Family Pass. She can go to the front of line and get on the WhirlyFunRide any time she wants.

Today it felt like the right thing to do. And it would have been, if she hadn't been so set on riding that she broke the rules and stayed on after LAST CALL.

Not me, she said to herself when the horn blew. *Nobody tells me what to do.* When her capsule hit the platform, she hid under the seat until the attendant slapped the door shut and the wheel moved on to let the people in the last few cars get out.

Soon she was the only passenger on the WhirlyFun-Ride.

Everything moved faster after that.

The car sped along, back into the whirly part and up

the roller coaster and down the water chute. Jule was howling with excitement as her car came up the last peak and clicked into its slot for the spin on the Ferris wheel that brought you down to earth. She wanted it to go again. Again.

Then the wheel shuddered and stopped for the night.

The lights in the car went out. Jule was stuck at the top.

She yelled and banged but a hundred yards below, the attendants were busy shutting down. Frustrated, she tried to open the glassy door so she could throw something. She'd do anything to get their attention, but the capsule was shut tight. The overhead lights went out. "Don't go," she shouted, even though there was no point.

Foolish as it was, she tried willpower: *Find me.* As if that would work. The workers are gone. MegaMall Security stops patrolling after the mall shuts down. They're watching on banks of monitors in locked offices somewhere far away from here. Besides, on camera one kid waving and pounding at the top of a ride is no more than a speck, even if you happen to be looking.

Except for a string of work lights at the base of the giant ride, the amusement plaza is dark. It's long past closing. The crystal chandeliers are set to *dim* and the last attendant has left.

She is stupendously alone.

If only she hadn't lost that phone! OK, she lost it at the skating rink where she wasn't supposed to be in the first place, which is how she and Aunt Christy got into the fight. Even people who love each other get mad and say stupid things. It happens, you know?

It's late. She's beyond hungry. The air in her tightly sealed prison is getting stale.

To cheer herself, Jule pulls out the brand-new Maglite she bought when late afternoon sunlight still played on the crystal dome. The beam is tiny but powerful. Lying on her back, she aims it up into the great glass dome above the Ferris wheel. She is cheered by its tiny reflection in the gently curving glass. It glints like a new star. She wedges the miniature flashlight into her shoe and aims it at the sky. It is shining upward long after she drops into sleep.

Why not sleep? Until the morning cleanup crews arrive, she's alone.

Or she thinks she is.

Jule Devereaux has no way of knowing that there are figures stirring in the deep shadows far below. In the shadows, even denser shadows move. Two swift, dark shapes course back and forth in the courtyard of the abandoned amusement park. Quick and ravenous, the scavengers slouch along, scooping up half-eaten candy bars, small change, lost wallets and forgotten toys. Anything they can't eat they will take back to their leader, who . . .

Distracted by a reflected light, one of the intruders looks up. The silence is punctuated by an ugly hiss. "Ssssst!"

The other looks up to where he is pointing. A rush of air escapes him like poison gas. "Hsssss!"

Together, the two scavengers spit and mutter, consulting. Then they turn as one, and like a pair of hunting ferrets they slither out of the courtyard of the amusement plaza and into the uncharted corridors beyond, hissing with excitement as Jule sleeps on.

TWO

ELSEWHERE IN THE MEGAMALL Tick Stiles says in a low voice, "What's the first rule here?"

"Keep your head down," Jiggy says.

"And the second?"

Jiggy says grudgingly, "If you see anybody, lie low."

Tick turns to the others, who have formed a circle around them. Dutifully, the night children repeat: "If you see anybody, lie low."

"And you did . . . What?"

Jiggy snarls, "Got in a fight."

"You mean, *started* one."

They are coming down to it now. Tick motions to the others, and the little band of lost and abandoned children that he's collected backs off so he can finish this. Being in charge isn't anything he wanted, but the night children depend on him. After all, he's lived in the mall longer than anyone. He's been here forever, so he knows what to do. He takes care of them. His kids have places to stay and plenty to eat and he keeps them safe. He's even given his ragtag band of stray children a name, to make them proud.

But Jiggy doesn't care. "No way, it was their fault!"

The Castertown Crazies back away so Tick can have it out with Jiggy. He clamps a hand on the scruffy boy's shoulder. "Admit it."

"No way. The Dingos started it," Jiggy whines. Chronic troublemakers, Jiggy and his little sister Nance blundered out where they shouldn't, and stirred up the Dingo tribe.

Now, the Dingos are new to the Castertown Mega-Mall; they've only been here since Christmas. With dozens of sectors in the sprawling MegaMall to choose from, Burt Arno's gang of blustering misfits with their home-made tattoos and showy nose studs blundered into the one sector of the MegaMall that Tick and his friends have occupied and protected for years.

It poses a huge security risk.

Burt and his gang rolled into the courtyard with no idea what would happen if they got caught. The first Tick knew of it was a mix-up in the Montecassino food court near closing time. Ten minutes more and Burt's Dingos would have brought mall Security down on them. Tick and his main men came out of the shadows and dragged Burt and his henchmen behind the counter at Panda Express. They clamped hands over the outsiders' mouths and grappled them to the floor. It was a struggle but they kept the Dingos quiet until Security had come and gone.

It took a lot of parleying to make Burt see the point because the leader of the Dingos is by no means the smartest bear in the woods. Grimly, Tick taught Burt that to survive in the Castertown MegaMall, his Dingos had to stay out of sight.

"Kids they catch," Tick warned, "end up in the State Home."

"In your face," Burt growled. "We just broke out. No way are we going back!"

"Then keep down and keep quiet," Tick said. "Don't bother us and we won't bother you."

Grumbling, Burt Arno agreed to the pact.

Things went along OK after that. Tick hates having another gang in his sector, but it's a big place. A war with the Dingos would destroy everything and everybody he's worked so hard to protect. But now. Now!

Now idiot Jiggy and his wild sister have brought the Dingos out like hornets. Jiggy snarls, "They started it."

Tick says grimly, "Whose fault is that?"

"I'm sorry!" The kid's purple hair is smeared with thick black guck so ugly that there's no telling what it is. Standing at Jiggy's elbow, his little sister is trying not to cry. Nance has tufts sticking up where her braids used to be. Somebody hacked off her hair with a kitchen knife. A warning from the Dingos, Tick supposes. It's only the first.

"Sorry isn't enough. Look." Tick is holding a note.

Montecassino Courtyard at 3 a.m.
Or else.
Come alone. Turn out your pockets.
Stand empty and hope I show myself.
Burt Arno, leader of the Dingo Tribe

"It was Jigg's idea," Nance sniffs. She's trying to pretend she doesn't care about the braids, but her whole face is quivering.

Big mistake, adopting these two, Tick thinks. They're nice enough, careless but well meaning, but they're not like the rest of his night children, ordinary kids who got lost in the monster mall and were too little and helpless to find their way back. Tick wants to help, but everybody knows what Security does with lost children. They end up in the State Home. The smalls miss their parents; some of them still cry in the night.

These two, on the other hand, are runaways, and tough ones at that. Jiggy and Nance are older than most of the lost and abandoned children Tick shepherds here in the echoing Romanesque-themed sector of the tremendous mall. Nance is thirteen, and Jiggy's almost as old as Tick.

They have changed everything with one stupid act.

Until tonight, Tick's little band was safe in their sector of the sprawling complex. There are other gangs, he knows, in outlying areas, but they keep to themselves.

Until tonight, he and his Crazies lived quietly, far below Security's radar; nobody knew they were here.

Now Jiggy and Nance have brought the Dingos down on them, and Security? It's only a matter of time.

The two of them weren't being malicious, lacing the lobby of the sector's 3D/360 Megaplex with loops of monofilament— after all, the place is supposed to be deserted, right? They stuck their heads into the biggest movie house, yelling, "FIRE!" The Dingo Tribe came boiling out. Two dozen Dingos hurtled into the lobby and got fouled in yards and yards of transparent fishing line. Flailing Dingos tripped and crashed on the marble, all but Burt Arno, who took out after Jiggy and brought him down. Instead of beating the salt out of the pair, he rubbed crank case oil in Jigg's hair, sawed off Nance's braids and sent them home with this note.

"You know what this means." Scowling, Tick shakes out the red blanket that signals: WAR COUNCIL.

Where they had been jabbering and laughing, excited to go out and play in the nighttime mall, the Castertown Crazies drag bedrolls and pillows into the circle and sit down facing Tick. Scruffy in T-shirts and baggy jeans, ragtag outfits assembled from mall castoffs, they wait. They watch Tick with white, white faces. It's been years since anybody here has been out in the sun. Nobody who lives here and wants to stay here without getting caught goes out in broad daylight in the Castertown MegaMall. It's Tick's job to keep his people fed and safe and out of sight, and now Jiggy and Nance have put everything at risk.

"War," kids mumble uncertainly.

Tick says, "Not if I can help it."

"Look what they did to me." Jiggy's voice zigzags. "We have to fight!"

"No. We have to make a plan."

A war council is the last thing Tick wants to have right now, but here they are. The little band is his to take care of because he's the oldest. He's lived in the MegaMall from the beginning. He was here even before Opening Day. Ask Tick Stiles what happened and he'll say it's none of your business, when the truth is, he doesn't exactly know. He was five, he came in with his mom and dad for the Employee Preview Party, the big gold card from Zozzco got the Stiles family into the pre-opening celebration be-cause his parents did some of the most important blueprints for the MegaMall and this was the mysterious Mr. Zozz's way of saying thanks.

There was silver lettering and Mom read it aloud. As a special thanks for all their hard work on the project, designers, builders and their families would have the run of the mall.

Before it opens. Dad's face was shining. Mom beamed. They loved him. They were pleased and proud. *What an honor. What a treat!*

THIS IS HOW TICK got a seat in the Tiny Train for the inaugural ride. Grownups were too big for the caboose so Mom and Dad stood back, smiling and waving as the attendant strapped him in. When the train stopped after the first circuit of the amusement plaza and Tick got out, both of his parents were gone. First he thought it was a mistake. So many other children were getting off and going home with their families that nobody noticed one leftover boy. Tick called and hunted and hunted and called. Then he wandered the plaza until night fell and the place emptied out.

Dad had taught him, If you get lost, stay in one place so we can come back and find you, so Tick settled down in the MegaMall to wait. He never guessed it would be years. How did he know to stay out of sight? He couldn't tell you. He only knew that Zozzco Security was not here to help him. He saw what they did to a couple of kids who went crying for their parents. They caught them in nets and dragged them away. *These people are bad.* Small as he was, he hid out in a furniture store near the food court; there were so many half-eaten dinners and abandoned pizzas that he never went hungry.

Over the years Tick ate, he read, he looked at videos and listened in on the grownups talking in the MegaMall, a hundred thousand strangers with a million ideas— interesting!— and the more he looked and listened, the more he learned.

Tick Stiles hasn't spent a day in school since he got lost but unlike Burt Arno, he is sharp. Things that kids like Burt can spin out lifetimes not learning, Tick knows.

Mom and Dad have been gone for so long now that he's forgotten what they look like. He misses them, but in a strange, abstract way, like a wonderful idea he used to have and forgot.

The MegaMall is his home and family now. It's been ten years. Over time Tick has found others— children who were lost or accidentally left behind or quite simply ditched by grownups who were sick of taking care of them; runaways, like Jiggy and Nance. He works hard to keep his little band well fed and comfortable and safe, but now . . .

The meeting is over. James, who's been here almost as long as Tick, says, "So, we have to lie low for a while."

Tick says uneasily, "I hope that's all we have to do."

The small ones shift and grumble because they know what's coming. It's what they have to do every time they're threatened with exposure, and the Dingos present a huge threat. They like this hideout. Nobody wants to move.

Willie Haskell, who in the lineup of old-timers in the Crazies living under cover has been here almost as long as James, asks, "What are we going to do?"

"Not sure," Tick says. "Depends. Nance, were you guys followed?"

She shakes her head.

"Jigg?"

"No!"

"You sure?"

Jiggy's voice rises. "I told you, no!"

Somebody says, "Yeah, like you'd even notice, you're so dumb."

Somebody else says, "You never should have showed yourself in the first place."

"We didn't show ourselves." Jiggy says, louder, "We didn't! It happened. I'm sorry, OK?"

"Quiet," Tick says. "Keep it down."

Somebody else mutters, "Like he even knows how."

A girl says, "What ever happened to *Lie low*?"

This is the story of their lives here.

Lie low? It's the rule.

The Castertown Crazies don't go out in the daytime. Go out when there are shoppers and clerks around and you start looking maybe a little too familiar. Clerks and daytime Security men see you and after a while they start to remember: *What, you here again?* Once they recognize you, somebody's going to figure out just exactly who you are.

No. That you are here too often. Like, all the time.

That you don't have a home they can send you back to; you live here, in the Castertown MegaMall. When you're living on your own in a place where nobody is supposed to be living at all, you can't afford to attract attention. If grownups find you they will come at you with social workers. The State Home.

The night children sleep in the day and play after hours. By night they can do anything they want in the halls and courtyards, as long as they take care. Avoid the cameras. Keep it down. They can have footraces over the bridges or run their bikes down the marble stairs, but even the most disciplined kids get restless.

Long, quiet days in the hideout get on their nerves.

Somebody decides on the spur that he's hungry or she needs something: "I'll only be gone a minute." "It's almost closing time." "Come on, Tick, it's a big mall. Who's going to notice one more kid?"

Then they come skidding back into headquarters with mall Security on their tails and Tick and the others have to grab what they can and scatter until it's safe.

The colony is always on the move.

In a place where businesses open and close overnight and new businesses take their time moving in, this isn't hard. For now, the Castertown Crazies are living in the big empty space left by Sligo Sporting Goods, a store that went bankrupt overnight. There wasn't even time for a clearance sale. Management left behind a rack of fleeces, some tents and an entire case of sleeping bags. It's the best place Tick and his colony have found so far, and the most comfortable he's been since he was five years old and living at home.

Like all defunct businesses, the shell of the sports store is protected by a false front, so passersby won't see what's inside. The false front is painted to look like just another wall, instead of a store that has died. As long as the front is unchanged, Tick's colony is safe, but they're never comfortable anywhere for long.

One of these nights he'll go out and find a fresh sign:

COMING SOON
NEW BOUTIQUE/MUSIC STORE/
INTERNET CAFE

He always does. It always happens sooner or later, and Tick and his people have to move. The Dingos have just pushed up the deadline, is all. This, as far as Tick is concerned, is the downside of living here in the MegaMall. They never stay anywhere for long.

Still, it's little enough to pay for freedom. The freedom is intense.

From 10 p.m. when the cleaning crews leave until 8 a.m. when they come back, this endless tangle of escalators and balconies and bridges and food courts and marble courtyards is dead empty, except for Security guys sleeping in front of their monitors and the restless colonies of night children like this one, roving the Mega-Mall in sectors far from the one where the Castertown Crazies play.

There are no adults around to complain about roughness or language or razor scooters on marble, and nobody to tell them what to do. The Crazies can dance in the galleries and go wading in the fountain if they want to. They can do everything but flap their arms and fly. Tick has the guards' schedules by heart and as long as they do no damage and avoid the surveill cameras, the MegaMall is theirs. It's like being king of the world.

At this point Tick would want to make clear to you that the Castertown Crazies live off the land but they earn their keep. They scavenge, yes, but they never steal. If you live in a place where too many people come with too much money, you can make plenty feeding deposit bottles to the return machines. The big kids pick up a little money sweeping out various establishments for a few dollars at the end of the day as long as they're careful not to work for the same person twice. There's the occasional tip they get for helping overloaded shoppers carry their purchases to a monorail port and making sure all the packages make it on board. The rest they make up by collecting crumpled bills that fall out of distracted tourists when they have too many shopping bags and lose their grip on their change.

The money goes into a pot to buy milk and other necessaries for the smalls. Tick knows it's better to travel light but when you run into a lost child you do what you can, particularly when it's somebody too little to take care of himself.

Right now he and the others are looking after tiny Doakie Jinks and Jane, at least until their parents come back for them.

It's a good life. All they have to do is avoid the cameras; no problem. After closing the Security guards hole up in glass booths. They make one round of the corridors at the final bell. Then it's back to the booth. They love to doze in front of their monitors, munching curly fries, half-watching their dizzying banks of TV screens.

Dodge Security and the cameras and the Crazies can do anything they want— or they could until the Dingos moved in on them a few months ago, disrupting everything. They came roaring out of their lair the first night they moved in here and brought out Security.

After the Crazies yanked them off the scene, Tick and Burt faced off in the service corridor. "You can't stay. You almost got us all caught."

"Why should we go?" Burt was too stupid or too lazy to colonize a new place. He set his meaty jaw, snarling, "You go."

Tick knows when to push and when to lay back. He asked, "You think you know where the surveill cameras are, what brings Security out, all that?"

"Um." Burt blinked. *No idea.* "Um."

"OK. Keep down, keep your people quiet and you can hang in until you learn. Deal?"

"Deal." And it was, until tonight. Now he wants to force Tick out in the open so he can have his stupid confrontation and, right. Bring Security down on them.

Studying the circle of faces, Tick considers. Stay in this hideout they've grown to love, or go before Burt catches up with them? His head lifts. There's a sound outside— too slight to be noticed by anybody but Tick. With a wave, he silences the others. He goes to the opening and slips out. In seconds, he's back. He is holding something, but the others are too stirred up to notice.

Jiggy whines, "So are you going to fight the Dingos or what?"

James asks in a low voice, "Are you going to do this meeting?"

"I have to. After we get everybody safe in a new place. Look." Tick is holding a red cardboard arrow. "The Dingos nailed this to the door."

James groans. "To bring Security down on us."

Tick nods. "Pack it all up. We're moving out."

So the sad little procedure begins. Kids deciding how much they can carry. Kids making piles of things they can take and sighing over things they will have to leave behind. They shrug on favorite clothing— knitted caps, extra shirts, stuffing their pockets with necessaries like soap and underwear and favorite toys.

They are lined up to move out when Willie says, "Wait!"

Alarmed by his tone, Tick turns.

"I just counted noses." Willie grimaces. "Doakie's gone."

THREE

CURLED UP IN HER glass capsule halfway between the ground and the sky, Jule drifts between sleep and consciousness while memories flicker like movies on the back wall of her head.

High above, far below and all around her, the Mega-Mall sprawls where there used to be nothing but empty prairie and a dying town. With Aunt Christy gone, she'd just as soon be here as anywhere, safe in the heart of her second home.

There are weird things about the MegaMall, she knows, but in addition to being the brightest spot in the flat prairie landscape, the tremendous shopping compound with its domes and spires saved the citizens of poor old Castertown.

In the old, old days people used to flock to Castertown to buy cedar chests. Everybody was happy and everything was fine. Then cedar chests went out of style. They kept rolling out of the factory all the same, but Castertown sold fewer and fewer every year. Unwanted cedar chests piled up in the warehouse by the river until there wasn't room for even one more. Workmen piled the extras on a giant bonfire. The factory closed. Overnight, the whole town was out of a job.

Jule lived at home with a real mother and father back in those days. Mommy and Daddy designed cedar chests. After the factory closed, they patched their clothes and ate what they could afford. They didn't have much but Jule had Mommy and Daddy and everything was fine. Then a black Learjet landed in the middle of the bleak prairie and changed history.

On the anniversary of the Grand Opening, they still show the Zozzco documentary in all the Castertown schools.

In the video, a frame comes up: THE FIRST DAY.

First there is nothing but the prairie. Then the Learjet lands. A white limousine and four black ones roll down ramps into the open plain. They are bringing officials of the Zozzco Corporation to City Hall.

There is a drumroll. Isabella Zozz steps out of the white limousine. The high collar of her white uniform is studded with diamonds. There are six wide gold stripes on the right sleeve. The cameras follow her into the mayor's office, where she makes a speech. She brings an offer from her father, the rich and mysterious Amos Zozz.

It will make the city rich.

How could we refuse?

The grownups won't say exactly what Amos asked for in return, not even today. Well, there was rights to the entire prairie, but that isn't the whole thing. Nobody will say how, but the whole town is involved. The Town Council went to night meetings that nobody talked about. They signed secret papers. The Casterown MegaMall popped up on the prairie like a great glass city. Now everybody is rich, or most people are.

Nobody has ever seen Amos Zozz, and people say there are good reasons. Instead, a portrait of swanky, energetic Isabella, his famous daughter, hangs in Town Hall.

Suddenly Jule's parents had all the money they needed. They were happy, making new designs for something that was a lot bigger than a cedar chest. They were in charge of a very special project for the MegaMall. They bought her a bunny fur coat with a matching muff. Every night they came home from work with presents. Aunt Christy moved back from New York City to look after Jule while Mommy and Daddy went off to their new jobs. Every grownup in Castertown was working around the clock, getting ready for the Grand Opening, which was on April sixth.

She remembers exactly because on April fifth her parents disappeared.

Noise woke her in the night. Outside, car doors were slamming, boom, boom, boom. The front door rattled. People came in. She heard them muttering in the front hall. Later she heard shouting. She woke up the next morning and Mommy and Daddy were gone. She kept asking where were they, what happened, what *happened,* until Aunt Christy cried, "Don't, honey. Please don't." She was fake-smiling, but Jule thinks Aunt Christy was afraid. Her eyes were red and weird. "Please stop crying."

Jule sobbed and sobbed. "I can't."

"Well, try. I'll take you someplace wonderful, I promise."

"I want Mommy."

"You'll love it. You'll see, if you'll just hush."

"I want Daddy."

"Shh, honey. Shhh." Aunt Christy hugged her too hard, rocking back and forth with her chin in Jule's hair. "Come on."

It's hard to keep your mind on anything when you're that small. They went to the Grand Opening. Jule had a bouquet of balloons tied to her wrist and she was crying with her mouth full of candy. She can still taste the peppermint running down. At the base of the WhirlyFun-Ride Aunt Christy hugged her and pointed up. "Look. Isn't it wonderful? Your mommy and daddy made the plans!"

"Mommy?" Jule whipped her head around. "Dad? Are they here?"

"Just look at the WhirlyFunRide, honey, and be proud."

"I want my . . ."

"Hush, sweetie," Aunt Christy said, and even at that age Jule could tell her aunt was being brave. "I'm your mommy now. Shush and when you're a big girl, we'll get into one of those nice glass cars on that great big ride, and go around and up and up, to the very top!"

Willful Jule threw back her head and bawled. "I want to go now!" She cried and cried. Men came. Aunt Christy had to put her on the WhirlyFunRide just to get her to stop. She got on the WhirlyFunRide and went up so high that she started to feel better. It was so exciting that for a minute, she forgot.

Then they hit the top. From the top she could see everything: the sky above, the prairie, the town beyond and, like dots crossing the massive park that led from the parking lot, the people flocking to the MegaMall. Astonished, she shouted, "I see them, I think I see them!" And she almost could.

"Shh," Aunt Christy said. "That's better. Sit down. Hush. Be good, and the mall will take care of you."

In a funny way, it has. She and her aunt still come out here whenever they can. Or they did until last weekend, when they had the fight. It was a stupid fight. They didn't make up before they went to bed the way you're supposed to, and when Jule woke up the next morning Aunt Christy was gone.

Maybe it's her fault, for losing the phone. Aunt Christy was so mad that she shouted, "This is the fourth cell phone I've paid for, Juliette, and it's the last. Do you know how much these things cost?"

She stuck out her lower lip. "It's only a phone!"

For no reason, her aunt's eyes filled up. "I have to keep track of you." Aunt Christy was so upset that she practically shrieked, "How am I supposed to take care of you?"

"You only use it to boss me around!"

Then her Aunt Christy got *very* weird. Her voice got low and urgent, as if she was scared to death somebody would overhear. "We have to stay in touch!"

Yeah, Jule thinks sleepily. Drowsing in the glass capsule, she forgets she isn't home in bed. *Yeah, right.*

Then she jolts awake. The great wheel is shaking— no it's not a dream, and it's not her imagination. It's . . . Wait! She sees the Maglite's reflection jiggling in the dome above.

Wait. There is something happening far below. Something or somebody is down there in the dark. She lies rigid, gripping the bench seat like a shipwreck victim clinging to a raft.

A jerk rattles the car as far below, machinery comes alive.

"What!" she shouts.

The big wheel starts to move.

Then she whispers, "Who?"

Should she be afraid or should she be glad somebody's come to rescue her?

Are they here to rescue her?

Who are they, and what do they want? She doesn't know. Frightened, Jule turns off the powerful pencil flash and kneels on the bench seat, peering out. At first she can't see what lies below. The wheel's too big, the capsule is too high. Then as her transparent car descends, she sees a ring of flickering lights bobbing at the base of the slowly turning wheel.

At this distance it's magical, like a fairy circle. Beautiful, unless it's the scariest thing she's ever seen. More lights come drifting in from the perimeter. Weaving like lazy fireflies, others join the circle around the platform where, one after another, the WhirlyFunRide capsules come to a stop.

Jule's mouth forms an O but no sound comes out. *Who?* Are they mall Security or a rescue party or what? What if she's blundered into some huge secret that somebody at Zozzco is trying to hide? What will they do to her? She's afraid to find out.

Stupid, leaving the Maglite on like a great big HELLO

sign. The people down below may not know who Jule is, but the light tells them somebody is here. She switches it off.

If she gets under the seat *right now;* if she lies on the floor, maybe they'll forget which capsule the light came from. Like, how can they be sure? For all the times she's ridden the giant wheel, Jule never thought to count how many cars there are. Too many to search, she thinks, and shudders because she has no idea who is searching, or what they want.

There are worse things than being stuck at the top.

Like coming down.

Light rakes the glass top of the little car and Jule gasps. The big wheel jolts as cars reach the bottom one by one and some unknown person who's not very good at machinery brings each car skidding to the platform. Doors open and slam. They're looking. They are looking for her.

Whoever they are, they are thorough. And they're taking their time. Jule's car sinks closer to the platform with every jolt. She hears voices and the angry slap as doors slam on empty cars.

What are they going to do, crack her out like a baby chick? Are they here to save her or arrest her or do they want to pick up a mallet and smash her like an egg?

Cram yourself under the seat, Jule Devereaux. Hide.

Then the car hits the platform and she gasps. The door pops open and cold air rushes in. Jule crouches, shielding her eyes against the glaring halogen lamp. Outside people are arguing.

Somebody growls, "Get out."

She sits up. Gulping, she says with dignity, "Get that thing out of my eyes."

Somebody bangs a fist into her shoulder. A man with a light voice— or a kid with a deep one— says, "Shut up and get out."

If you can't hide, be brave. Jule is trying hard for a ferocious scowl but she has no idea what her face is doing. With her head high, she gets out. Unsteady, she stands as proud as she can after hours on the bench seat. She takes a deep breath. When it comes out, Jule's voice is bigger than she is.

She snaps, "Identify yourselves."

Light blinds her. Somebody giggles. There is nasty snickering.

Brave, Mom and Dad would be proud of her for sounding so brave. Jule barks, "What do you want with me?"

FOUR

IT'S SCARY OUT, AND Doakie Jinks is running, running, running. The first thing he learned about living in the mall was how to keep track, so he can find his way back from anyplace. Tick taught him. Kids have to know.

He has to get home!

Hurry, they might be chasing you!

Ooops, silly. This way, not that way!

Right. Not that corner, right around *this* corner, and whatever you do, stay away from the Dark Hall. Up the down escalator, into *this* corridor. He almost has it memorized. Zigzag through the passage next to *that* store.

He has to get home in a hurry. He has to find Tick. He has to get Tick and tell him the trouble before anything worse happens. He has to tell him soon!

The trouble is, the corridors are long and the marble is slippery. Doakie's legs are short and he's so new here that when he turns a corner he isn't always sure.

He doesn't even know how come he's living here. He used to live in Dubuque with Mummy and Daddy, but then they broke up and Mummy moved to Castertown.

She got a job and signed Doakie up for kindergarten. He's starting next fall. Or he was.

He doesn't know what's going to happen to him now.

See, Doakie rode all the way out here on the shuttle with Mummy because she couldn't get Grace to babysit, even though Grace is her new best friend.

Well, he's seen all about the great stuff for kids in the mall on television, and he really wanted to come.

Besides, it was the last day of the midsummer fur sales and Mummy was desperate. So they got here, it feels like a long time ago, but he thinks it was only the other week. Mummy said be patient, this won't take long, she was just trying on coats. She said when they were done she would take Doakie to all the stores he wanted to see and get him a ticket on the WhirlyFunRide to make up for it. Now, that was before. See, Doakie's been living here in the MegaMall practically forever and he only just saw the big ride for the first time tonight.

If he knew where Doakie went, Tick would freak.

How Doakie ended up living here is, when they got to the fur store Mummy promised they wouldn't be long. She said sit here like a good boy, which he did, but the velvet bench was hard and she was taking forever. He got down and crawled around under the fur coat racks while Mummy tried on about a hundred dozen coats. He played like he was in the jungle making friends with tigers and bears but the fur coats weren't alive, not really, until he pulled one down off the hanger and got inside. Mummy petted his head when he crawled out and growled at her, but she hardly noticed. She was too busy twirling in front of the three-way mirror in coats, and asking the lady did this one make her look fat. It always did. Then she'd sigh and drop it on the pile. She was taking forever. Doakie got bored so he crawled into the big pile of coats and went to sleep.

The pile was warm and deep and cuddly, like a nest. Doakie slept and slept. When he woke up everything was dim and quiet, like the whole mall had gone to sleep too. The fur coat store was closed up for the night and everybody was gone. The store night-lights had turned everything pink.

It was so weird that he wasn't even scared.

He was starving to death so he took a baby box of chocolates from the pile of gold boxes the store gave away to every lady that bought a fur coat. Then he had to pee. There was a ladies' bathroom in the back of the store. Then he called for Mummy, just in case, but she wasn't there, he supposes she forgot because in the big fur jacket, he looked like just another coat. She would remember and come back, but it was taking too long. He ought to phone home and remind her but he doesn't know the number at their new house, plus he couldn't make the store phone work. After a while he found the night-delivery slot and wormed out, into the great big empty MegaMall.

When she didn't come he stood out in front of the fur store and called and called.

There were lots of rustles and echoes, that was all.

Then he sat down and cried and cried.

This big kid named Tick heard him crying, he sup-poses. Anyway, he looked up and all of a sudden Tick was there. This kid Tick is almost as tall as Daddy, but quick and skinny and nice. Light brown hair. He took Doakie by the hand so nicely that Doakie wasn't even scared. He said, "Shhshh. Chill, OK? And whatever you do, keep it down!"

All that was coming out of Doakie by that time was "Mmmmmmmm."

Tick didn't fuss, he just held Doakie's hand until he got quiet. Then he took Doakie to the Pirate Food Court and got him a soda and a hot dog still warm from the microwave, even though all the food stands were closed. Doakie was starving. When he got done eating he felt better. He stopped crying, at least.

"That's better," Tick said. "My name is Tick."

Then Tick asked him what happened and Doakie said.

Then Tick said, "You didn't tell me your name," and Doakie said.

Then Tick asked where he lived and Doakie burst into tears because he and Mummy just moved here and he doesn't know.

Tick got him a soft ice cream and waited until he quit hic-hic-ing. Then he handed it over and waited while Doakie ate it all up.

After that Tick got out this pocket computer thingy and turned it on. He said he was hacking into the system to find out if mall Security or the police had Doakie on the *Missing* list. He said he likes to help kids get back to their parents, but sometimes you just can't.

Doakie's name wasn't on any list, so Tick promised to take care of Doakie until Mummy came back or at least until she put his name on the *Missing* list.

Then he brought Doakie home to the hideout and introduced him to the other kids, so Doakie is a Castertown Crazy now, Tick says, at least for the time being, which means he has a job to do. He just saw something and he has to run as fast as he can. Something bad is about to happen, he just knows it. He has to tell Tick. So would you, if you saw somebody in trouble.

Tick will know what to do.

He has to tell Tick so Tick will come and save her.

It's what he does.

Doakie will probably get in trouble for sneaking out into the mall before Tick gave the All Clear, but maybe he'll be too distracted by Doakie's news to notice.

The thing is, there are bad kids in the mall. Everybody in the Crazies knows this, but tonight . . . Tonight Doakie saw them up close, and they're gonna do something awful. If Tick doesn't stop them, Doakie doesn't know what they're gonna do, but he knows. He just knows. They caught a girl, and they're gonna do something awful to her.

Did they see him before he ducked and skibbled out? He doesn't think so. He doesn't know.

Doakie is running hard, just in case. He keeps thinking he hears footsteps behind him but when he stops, they stop.

Gasping, he rounds yet another corner; he *does* hear footsteps. They're close and they're getting closer, but if he hurries, he can make it. If he can only make it he can . . .

He's running so fast that his feet slip out from under him and he falls down.

Ow!

This is it, Doakie thinks, scrambling up. *If they're gonna get me, this is when they're gonna get me.* Those are definitely footsteps following, but like lightning he dodges and rolls behind a pile of cartons that got delivered to the wrong store and prays whoever's chasing won't see the blood he drooled on the white marble floor out front when he fell.

Ug! The footsteps are still pounding toward him. They are getting closer and closer. Then when he's just about to die from not breathing, they stop.

FIVE

Trapped at the base of the WhirlyFunRide, Jule spins, trying to see past the glare of her captor's light. On the dark floor below the looming Ferris wheel, flashlights move in the dark— other people— kids, she thinks. How many are there anyway? She doesn't know. The one who pulled her out of the capsule is definitely the leader. That's all she knows.

The tough kid signals one of his followers. "Yo, Kirk."

A boy much bigger than Jule grabs her elbows from behind, frog-marching her off the exit platform. She struggles but he is too strong. Jule stands on the main floor with her bare face exposed, blinded by the work light the leader shines directly into her eyes. Everybody in the circle sees her, but she can't see them.

Her captor rumbles, "What are you doing here?" The voice is deeper than it should be, but this isn't a man. He sounds more like a boy whose voice has dropped too far. Crowding her, the others mutter and grumble but in the glare she can't make out how many, or who they are. "Answer me!"

"Nothing! I'm not doing anything!"

"Why were you hiding?"

"I wasn't hiding," Jule says. "I got stuck."

"Yeah, right," a girl says in a voice that's too big for the space. "So. Are you here to join us or turn us in?"

At least Jule thinks it's a girl. The question is confusing. "Join what?"

"No new members," someone snarls, and the others join in.

Blinded by the light, Jule blinks. "Members?"

"Shut up, Donny." The leader shoves the light so close that Jule's eyelashes curl in the heat. "Answer! What are you doing here?"

If only she could see! "I told you, nothing."

"Nobody comes in here for nothing. Now tell the truth."

Standing tall and proud as she can, Jule challenges him right back. "And what are you doing here?"

His voice grinds like stripped gears. "None of your rotten business."

But the girl with the big voice comes back with an answer. "We saw your light."

"Shut your hole, Mag."

"No, Burt. You shut up," Mag hisses. "Gotta find out who this person is."

"Watch your mouth or you better watch out, Margaret Sullivan," the burly leader says. "Nobody talks to Burt Arno that way."

"Except me." Laughing, Mag steps out of the circle and closes in on Jule. "OK, girl. Answer. What's your name?"

"Jule Devereaux." Jule tries to jerk free but Kirk's fingers clamp tighter. "I'm from town."

"Town!" Mag gives Jule a shove. "What are you doing here?"

"I told you, I'm not doing anything!"

"It doesn't matter what she's doing. She's seen us," Burt says. "She could turn us in."

Mag says patiently, "We need to find out what she's doing here so we'll know what to do. Now get that light out of her eyes."

"Thanks."

"Whatever." Mag leans in like a dentist getting ready to yank a molar. The girl's red hair is frizzed eight ways to Sunday and she's missing some teeth. "Now, what are we gonna do?"

Burt snaps, "I'll figure it out!"

"We need to know!" Angry, Mag peers into Jule's face. "Look, girl. Nobody hides out in here for no reason. Talk."

"I'm not hiding out, I got trapped." Jule knows how stupid she was, overstaying LAST CALL. "It was an accident!"

"Sure," Mag says sourly. "Sure it was."

"Really." She tries to smile. "I don't want to be here at all."

There is an ugly silence. It seems Jule has made a mistake.

"You don't want to be here?" Burt rumbles, "You don't want to be in here, you don't have to be here. Fine," he says in a new, hard voice that scares her more than she will admit. "Let's see what we can do about that." He turns to the group. "What are we gonna do with her?"

"Tar her," somebody suggests and the others chime in like a bunch of A students trying to make it to the head of the class.

"Shear her."

"No, snatch her baldheaded."

"Tie her up and throw her in the Peace Fountain."

"Tie her in front of the Dinky Train."

"Don't be stupid, get rid of her."

At Jule's back, Kirk gives her a shake. "Get rid of her for good and all!" His thick breath blasts the back of her neck. Every inch of her skin tightens.

Some kid says brightly, "Clearance sale!"

A girl in the circle purrs, "Drop her in the Trash Spinner."

The Dingos close in, pushing and shoving. Suggestions buzz like hornets, filling the air. "Underground tram tracks. The trams'll mash her flat."

"Zozzco offices."

"Shut up, stupid. Like you want *them* to know we're here?"

"Security headquarters."

"No way, she'd turn us in!"

Then somebody says, "The Dark Hall."

Everybody gasps. Whispers ripple and build as kids shift uneasily and close in on Jule, repeating, "The Dark Hall."

Suddenly everybody's afraid. "The Dark Hall."

Their tone chills Jule to the heart, two dozen boys and girls muttering, "Not the Dark Hall."

Burt shouts, "Enough!" Turning, he rakes his people with the light. "Dingos, back off!"

There is a rustle and a flurry as the shadows fall back. Whoever these Dingos are, they're used to taking orders.

"That's better. Now, quiet. I've gotta think."

In the long silence, Jule starts to sweat.

Kirk has been gripping Jule tightly for so long that his fingers are trembling. One sharp tug and she'd be free.

But Burt Arno is thinking, whatever that means. The dark shapes in the circle murmur and sigh restlessly. If she ran they would catch her in seconds, and Jule knows better than to try.

After too long, Burt says, "OK, Kirk, let her go."

Kirk lets go with a little grunt of relief.

It's like having a bearskin rug lifted off. Jule shakes her arms, waiting for the feeling to come back. Squinting into the light, she waits. Everybody in the circle around them waits. Jule doesn't run. She doesn't even cast around for an exit. The light is blinding; if Burt turns it off this very minute, afterimages will be flashing in her head for hours. It will be a long time before Jule can see what's out there or guess which way to run. Here under the dome at the end point of the fabulous WhirlyFunRide, time has stopped, at least for now.

Jule does not ask, *Can I go now?* She knows better. Hulking Burt Arno is thinking. It will go badly for anybody who interrupts.

Even Mag is still.

"OK," he says finally. "Let's do this."

Everybody sighs with relief.

"Tidgewell, Barlow, the shackles."

Two stringy boys about Jule's age close in with duct

tape and a Kryptonite bicycle lock. When they're done Jule's wrists are firmly taped to either end of the lock.

Somebody produces a bejeweled dog collar and new leash with Pet Parade labels still attached. Jule can't know that where the Castertown Crazies use castoffs or pay for everything they take in the MegaMall, the Dingos steal.

"OK, Mag. Grab the leash," Burt says. "We're moving out."

"Where to?"

"Where else?" Burt's ugly laugh makes Jule shiver. "The Dark Hall."

Somebody in the little cluster of followers moans on a high note. "Ooooh, noooo!"

Mag says sharply, "We're not going *in* there." It's half statement, half question.

"Who, us? No, not us," Burt says and he heads for the nearest red exit sign, pushing Mag and her captive along in front of him. Behind, the other Dingos fall in muttering, and the little group moves out. "We're not going in there," he says, and the air trembles as everybody but Jule lets out a sigh of relief. Burt adds, "She is."

SIX

TICK IS TRYING TO do three things at once.

First, he is organizing the move. He is worried about little Doakie but he needs to get his people to the next place and safely settled before he does anything else. Then he can find Doakie and get ready to meet Burt Arno for the big confrontation at 4 a.m.

Right now, he has to move. The deserted shell of Sligo Sporting Goods was a wonderful hideout for as long as it lasted, but that's all over now. Too bad. The place was big enough for everybody and stocked with a lot of cool things, including a hot plate and a pocket fridge left behind by the company when they went bankrupt and moved out. It was the best hideout they ever had, but they have to pack up what they can, and go.

Tick is scrawling on a pad, but his mind is on everything else. The smalls are busy bundling up bedrolls while Willie and James sort supplies into two piles: things they can take and things that are too bulky to take.

Jiggy and Nance are working away with their heads down, but the guilty look Jiggy shoots him says it all: *my fault.* Tick will have a sit-down with the two of them— tomorrow, probably, lay down some ground rules— but first he has to make it through tonight. They're leaving riches behind: extra clothes, camp chairs, pictures the kids drew, but in the world of the MegaMall, when you say goodbye to an object, something new will come along to take its place. He had the next spot picked out long before tonight, so that's taken care of. Tick's long life in the Mega-Mall has taught him to adapt. Every night he goes prospecting for new places, just in case.

Location is not the problem. Getting everybody there without being followed is.

He is busy making maps so the Crazies can go out one by one and find their way to the new hideout without getting lost. All but the smallest Crazies have to travel alone so they can filter into the vacant music store on the far side of the Pennsylvania Dutch Food Court in the music gallery without being seen. The newly vacated store isn't as big as Sligo Sports and it's a lot trashier, but it will have to do. The owners moved out so fast that they abandoned a drum set, a trumpet and a handful of CDs, which is a plus.

There is the problem of finding an abandoned CD player, but that can wait.

The second thing he has to do is figure out how to handle Burt Arno when they meet in the Montecassino courtyard. What does the leader of the Dingos want, an apology or Jiggy's head on a stick or something worse? He doesn't know. Of course he'll go alone, but will Burt be alone?

It wouldn't occur to him to go armed. Tick would never think of traveling with a weapon, no Swiss Army knives for him, no pellet guns and certainly not a baseball bat. His folks have been gone since he was five but he knows what would make them proud. It takes brains, not weapons to solve problems.

He's not that kind of person, but what kind of person is Burt? He is the wild card that Tick never thought he'd have to play.

Since that first meeting Tick has only seen the leader of the Dingos in passing— the wild glint in Burt's eyes as he and his Dingos swarmed past him on their way out— the chains, the savage flash of teeth. When they meet, Tick is fully prepared to say whatever Burt wants to hear, anything to make this pass. He'll apologize, if that's what it takes. Jiggy and Nance thought it was funny when they laid their trap for the outsiders' gang; they were laughing when they sprayed the Dingos with Silly String, but what they did was destructive and dangerous. It was also extremely dumb. He will apologize, but what if that isn't enough?

Tick is prepared to offer goods, like palmcorders from the Crazies' collection of objects left behind by careless shoppers, along with the tribe's complete supply of chocolate; he's even prepared to offer what little money the Castertown Crazies have saved, but is money enough?

The third thing, and this bothers him most, is what to do about Doakie Jinks. Kid's too young to read any note they might leave for him, and not smart enough to know the Crazies' code even if he could. Leaving a map for him would be dangerous. What if the Dingos or mall Security found it instead? Tick supposes they could just go on without him and hope for the best, but Doakie's not ready to take care of himself. He's just a little boy!

Gleaming red in the corner where he threw it, the Dingos' arrow taunts him.

They can't stay here one minute longer.

They can't just abandon Doakie to the mall.

Around him the Crazies have finished packing, stowing, loading up. Tick's people have their whole lives strapped to their backs. They clump together, shuffling expectantly.

One of the smalls clears his throat.

James murmurs, "Time for liftoff?"

Willie shakes his head. "No way. Search party first."

James says, "No time. We can't . . ."

"We have to send out a search party," Willie says doggedly.

"Aren't we gonna look for Doakie?" Doakie's best friend Jane tugs on Tick's elbow. She's trying not to cry.

"Can't," James growls. "We have to move!"

It's time for Tick to call the shot. "Both," he says. "We have to do both."

In the next second the vinyl flaps that protect the Crazies' secret door part so smoothly that at first even Tick thinks the change in the room is just a glitch in the air-conditioning, nothing more.

A deep voice says, "Lose somebody?"

Tick wheels. "Lance!"

Tall, rough-cut Lance the Loner has entered their headquarters so swiftly and quietly that even Tick didn't know.

The mysterious outsider stands at the opening in the ragged camo pants and jacket that make him look like a deserter from some unknown army. He's bigger than Tick. Older. As always, his face is covered by black wool that hides everything but the green eyes. He wears the ski mask because Lance the Loner is so private that nobody gets to see his face.

Lance has lived in the mall longer than anybody, even Tick, but he and Tick don't really know each other. They don't know each other even after all these years. They pass, not like strangers, exactly, but like orbiting planets that never meet. From the beginning, Lance kept to himself. He comes and goes so quietly that you don't even know that he's been.

The two don't talk, but Tick thinks of the Loner as a friend. He finds notes left by Lance sometimes: where the best food is. Which part of the sector to avoid, and why. When this happens he goes through the Crazies' stores of food and clothes and small electronics and leaves a present out for Lance. The thank-you gifts are never acknowledged, but when Tick comes back to the spot to check, they're always gone.

He sees at once what Lance is doing here. He has a squirming bundle tucked under his left arm.

"Doakie!"

"They almost got him." The big boy drops Doakie on the floor. Doakie wheezes, trying to get his breath.

Willie says, "What did you do to him?"

"Saved his hide." Lance snorts. "A Security goon almost got him. You should be more careful of your kids."

"I just found out he was missing."

"My point."

James says, "He just slipped out."

Something about the Loner makes Willie all defensive. "We were about to go looking for him, OK?"

Syllables come popping out of Doakie: "T-t-t . . ."

"What's the matter, Doak?" Tick kneels. "Are you choking or what?"

Doakie's eyes are bulging with excitement. He has something to tell but he is wheezing so hard that he can't talk.

Tick looks up. "What happened? Is he OK?"

"He'll be fine," Lance says. "Just got the breath knocked out of him."

Doakie is waiting for his chest to inflate so he can speak. Struggling, he tries, "Tuh . . ."

"Where was he?"

"Tuh . . ."

"Cartons outside Latrobes Luggage."

"Tuh . . . huh . . . ick!"

"Security bearing down on him, fast."

"Did they see you?"

Lance's head comes up: proud. "No. I'm too good. Sorry about the can't-breathe thing. I had to get him out fast."

"Duh . . ."

"Take it easy, Doakie. Don't try to talk." Tick stands. "So, Lance. Thanks!"

Doakie sputters, "Duh . . ."

"Shh, Doak."

"Duh . . ."

"Really, Lance. Thanks!"

It's hard to tell what Lance is thinking because of the ski mask, but Tick thinks he's grinning. It shows up in the little bounce in his voice. "Welcome. It's no big."

This is the most conversation they've ever had.

"Dingos!" Doakie manages at last. With a whissshhhh, all the little boy's breath comes rushing back into him.

Tick looks down, rummaging in his pockets. "Sports compass they left behind at Sligo Sports. Not really a present, but it's the least I can . . ."

When he looks up, the big loner is gone.

"OK, guys. Let's go. I'll bring Doakie."

"N-noooo!"

"It's OK, you're not too heavy, Doak. Now, let's move out!" Tick bends to collect Doakie and is surprised by a rush of words that comes out in a mixture of hot breath and spraying spit. "No it isn't," Doakie cries.

"What?"

"The Dingos caught a girl in the WhirlyFunRide," he says so fast that the rest comes out before Tick can slow him down or stop him to ask questions. "We have to go save her. Hurry. Before they hurt her bad!"

SEVEN

GOING ALONG WITH HER hands taped to the klunky bike lock and Mag running up her heels, Jule happens to be the only one looking up as the Dingos forge on. Mag grips her hair, jerking her head back so that she can only look up.

The others are looking straight ahead, down the long corridor that will, Jule supposes, take her into the next sector, like it or not. The Dingos are tromp-tromp-tromping, heading for the Dark Hall. She could call for help, but what's the point? She could scream until Sunday and no one would hear. The Casterbridge MegaMall is deserted. Metal grilles cover everything they pass, and on the long second-floor balconies, all the stores are closed.

It is scary and exciting. The gleaming corridors of the MegaMall are dead empty, with only store dummies watching from their windows. The Dingos have marched her through so many sectors that Jule loses count. Nobody speaks and she isn't about to ask. All she knows is that they are marching her to the Dark Hall.

Burt Arno is walking point. Burt's people turn when he turns; they go where he goes. When a surveill camera sweeps in their direction he hisses, "Freeze!" and the Dingos drop, crouching until the roving red eye hits the end of its arc and it's safe to move.

"So," Jule murmurs, "a moving target is harder to hit?"

"No," Mag spits. "A moving target is easy to spot!"

Wow, she answered me, Jule thinks. *If only we can talk.* She tries again. "Um. How far is it?"

Mag gives her hair a ferocious yank. "Don't ask."

Grouped in a tight triangle, the Dingos trot along behind Burt Arno like troops closing ranks to invade Mars. On either side of Jule, ahead of her and behind her, boys march with their heads down, walking the Burt Arno walk. Like their leader, they keep their heads down and their elbows tight to their sides— all but Mag, who grips Jule's hair, jerking her head back so that she can't help but look up, at the glossy railings of the second-floor balconies. Big and small, the others rush on, glaring out from under clenched eyebrows in a conscious imitation of Burt. The Dingos are on the move. They are so used to following orders that nobody stops to question their destination.

Nobody says what everybody is thinking.

The Dark Hall?

Burt wants us to go to the Dark Hall?

Yes, the Dark Hall.

Oh, noooooo. Not the Dark Hall.

You heard what he said. We all did.

OK, we're going to the Dark Hall.

Nobody is OK with it, but what Burt says, the Dingos do.

Jule, of course, is something else. She is a prisoner. The

Dingos are rushing her along to a place so scary that Caster-town kids talk about it in whispers, the way they talk about zombies and witches, or certain ghosts.

Everybody's afraid of the Dark Hall because nobody knows what it is or what happens there. In the Castertown MegaMall, somewhere in this monstrous, impenetrable honeycomb, one sector lies unexplored. Nobody goes there, but don't go looking for it. You won't come back. Even talking about it is dangerous.

If there is a Dark Hall.

Even though they make their parents bring them to the mall every chance they get, every girl and boy in Castertown is afraid of the Dark Hall. The Dark Hall is mysterious and terrible, like the Black Hole of Calcutta or the principal's office or the seventh circle of hell.

What goes on inside? Does Amos Zozz, who nobody has *ever seen* keep prisoners in the Dark Hall? Conduct weird experiments? Breed tremendous, scary animals or monsters or gigantic poison snakes? Is he building engines of destruction, or robots that will conquer the world? Nobody knows.

Teachers who can't control their classes threaten: "One more word and it's the Dark Hall for you." Even the most loving parents bring it up sometimes: "Bed. Now. You know what happens to children who disobey."

They don't, really, which is the scariest part of all.

At recess, they share rumors. "You heard what happened to Patty, right?"

"Mom says she moved."

"No way. She disappeared into the— you know."

Everybody shudders. "The Dark Hall?"

Someone whispers, "And they never saw her again."

It's weird. Step up and ask them what happens in the Dark Hall and even your parents will look you in the eye and say, "Don't be silly." They say flatly, "There is no Dark Hall."

Yeah, right.

We know there is a Dark Hall, but we can't prove it. The MegaMall is just too big to explore. Built like a gigantic honeycomb with six-sided galleries connected by circular courtyards with fountains, with hexagonal food courts filling the spaces between, the MegaMall is so expansive that nobody has walked the perimeter. For one thing, the honeycomb is still expanding. Cranes stand just beyond the finished walls. It would take an expedition weeks to map the finished areas, or so the grownups claim.

Besides, the parts you can visit are so exciting that you could spend a year and never see them all. What's more, all those shoppers have made the town so rich that the grownups don't really want to know what Amos Zozz is doing in the hall nobody sees. They shrug and look the other way, and the kids?

There's a lot of great stuff out there! We all grow up on the Zozzco jingles, singing along with MegaMall commercials on TV. "Spring and summer, winter, fall," they sing, "Cool kids shop at the MegaMall." Everybody who is anybody knows the dance. Everybody who matters has a ZZ T-shirt. Everybody who wants to be *somebody,* that is. Kids collect MegaMall coupons and free passes for rides in the amusement plaza by the hundreds every time you buy a ZZ Happy Burger or a ZZ Shake you get one. Obey the commercials and beg your mom to buy the special

Zozzco Crackle, and you'll find two in the box. The cereal is made right here in Castertown!

Aren't we all wearing Zozzco sneakers and doesn't everybody want ten more pairs of ZZ jeans?

Oh, there are other brands, but no kid wants them because every kid knows that ZZ makes the newest, hottest things. All the ads and commercials tell us so! As for our moms and dads, nobody wants to tangle with the corporation. Leave Zozzco alone and the money will keep pouring in.

Everybody says whatever happens, smile and don't ask questions. Grownups don't ask. They hated being poor.

If there's anything weird going on out there in the unknown sector of the MegaMall, the grownups of Castertown don't want to know. Nobody wants to upset the mysterious, powerful Amos Zozz. They're afraid of him. Jule's seen it in Aunt Christy's face. Ask the grownups and they'll deny it, but the children know.

Say the wrong thing and they might end up in the Dark Hall. Awful things happen there. The place is haunted. No, worse. The danger is mystical. The Dark Hall swallows every kid foolish enough to come near, and the Dingos are dragging Jule Devereaux toward the dark sector, step by step.

You bet Jule is scared.

All the Dingos are scared.

Even Burt Arno is scared, Jule can see it by the way his head is shaking as the hair rises on the back of his neck. She has to wonder what he has in mind for her. Does he just want to get rid of her, or is he planning some kind of sacrifice to the owner of the Castertown MegaMall? She doesn't know.

Scared or not, Burt's Dingos go thudding along in their work boots with their breath exploding in a steady *huh-huh-huh*. Jule has no idea whether they're close to their destination or whether they will have to trot along like this all night. She's just glad the thud-thud of two dozen pairs of feet and the *huh-huh-huh* of two dozen Dingos breathing in unison drown out the slight, constant rustle that she hears overhead.

The sound started as they rounded the first fountain and set off down the first corridor into the next sector, and it hasn't stopped. Jule hears, but the Dingos are too intent on where they are going to notice. The sound keeps pace with them, never louder, never fading, slight but incessant. The gang forges on without question but Jule's eyes snap wide. She is listening.

It is coming from the balcony above.

Holding her breath so she can hear better, she identifies soft footsteps overhead. Somebody on the second-floor balcony is keeping pace with them. She knows better than to stop. If she does anything at all, the Dingos will see. She can't tell who's moving along up there, but someone is following them. She sees a single shadow, loping along. As she watches other shadows fall in line, following the first. Soon there are many running along the balcony above her so silently that nobody but Jule Devereaux even guesses that Burt Arno's little regiment is not alone.

Jule has no idea who the strangers are, but she thinks they came in peace. Otherwise, wouldn't they attack? If she warned Burt or Mag that their Dingos were being followed, would they be so grateful to her that they'd let her go?

If Burt sent his tribe running after the intruders and they tangled, could she slip away during the fight? She isn't sure. She glances up, hoping for a signal, and to her surprise a tall, good-looking boy with tousled hair shows himself for a split second— just long enough to flash her a beautiful grin.

Oh, she thinks, looking at him for a few seconds too long, and in her astonishment, she breaks stride. *Oh!*

Mag yanks her back to attention and the little bunch of Dingos trots on.

When she looks again, he is as good as gone.

The Dingos are making good time until the red eye of the next surveill camera completes its arc and begins the inevitable swing back their way. Time to duck. The little platoon has done this so often on this march that Jule knows the drill.

Get down.

Burt Arno crouches with one hand raised: *silence.* Behind him, the Dingos halt and crouch in a perfect imitation. Hissing, Mag jerks Jule's hair and because she has no choice, Jule crouches too.

As before, they will be perfectly still as the eye of the camera plays on the little formation on the corridor floor, sees no movement, and moves on. *Crazy,* Jule thinks, freezing with the rest. Why don't the guards watching the surveill screens see two dozen kids playing statue? Why don't they swarm out of their booth to investigate?

A moving target is easy to spot?

She doesn't know.

In the next stupendous second, she does.

On the upper level, where Jule's unknown allies have

followed the Dingos silently, keeping low, everything changes. They move out into the lights. Kids of all sizes and ages leap into action on the balcony, flapping everything from beach towels and starters' flags to bath mats to inflatable baby ponds at the mean red eye of the camera, waving and shouting, trying every trick they can think of to get the attention of the MegaMall's guards. Hanging far out over the balcony rail, boys and girls jump up and down madly, like animal shelter puppies begging to be picked up, advertising: **Children here**.

A siren shrieks.

Advertising! Her unknown friends and their black-haired leader are trying to bring out the guards.

Just as quickly, they vanish.

Now she understands. Somebody up there risked exposure to bring down Security on the Dingos. For her? It's a kind of rescue, she supposes. It is! This rangy, handsome friend that Jule didn't even know she had just did something crazy. He and his gang just did everything but send up fireworks to alert the MegaMall guards, and she can't help thinking they did it to save her. Whatever they were thinking, it worked.

At the far end of the corridor, double doors fly open and a Security squad bursts out in black helmets and black uniforms, raking the corridors with high-intensity lights. Armed with bats and swinging weighted nets, they stand poised, deciding which way to go.

Right, she thinks. If you want to get people's attention, yell and wave!

The little display on the balcony caught somebody's eye up there in the Security booth, where nothing ever changes on the dozens of screens the Zozzco guards are paid to watch. In corridors where no outsiders come after closing time, any movement is like a red flag. Whether most of the guards were asleep or eating or playing cards or talking on the phone, *somebody* saw the commotion and hit the alarm.

Her secret friends have brought out the guards.

When she next looked up, they were gone. Smart!

What the guards see, thundering out, is Burt's unruly tribe. Trapped in the searchlights, Burt and his Dingos squawk, falling all over themselves in a mad attempt to escape.

As for her allies on the balcony? It's as if they don't exist.

Thudding along in shiny black boots, the Zozzco Security guards advance, closing in on Burt Arno and his scruffy Dingos with their leather jackets and their sad little tattoos and tarnished studs.

A voice booms out of hidden speakers, "DON'T MOVE."

Dingos scatter.

"STAND FAST."

Burt's Dingos run like coyotes from a pride of lions, leaving Jule Devereaux frozen in the empty corridor, helpless and alone.

"STAY WHERE YOU ARE."

Ordinarily she'd be glad to see Security coming, at least she thinks she would, but these Zozzco guards look mean. Evil. Dangerous. They advance with visors down and bats raised. Boot heels sound in double time: Clack-clack. Clack-clack. They begin to trot.

Even at this distance Jule is terrified. She wants to run,

but the unwieldy metal bike lock securing her hands knocks over a trash barrel and she almost falls.

The guards break into a run. Jule can't decide whether to turn and face them or drop on her belly and let them tramp right over her. She doesn't know what to do!

Then she hears a harsh, low voice.

"This way."

"Where?" Crazily, she spins, looking here, there. "Where?"

"Over here." Somebody smacks the overturned trash barrel and rolls it into a half turn, so the barrel lies between Jule and the oncoming guards like a protective wall.

Instinctively, she drops to the floor. "Where?" She doesn't see. She doesn't see!

"Here!"

Then she does see. A brass grate in the floor slips aside, revealing a narrow opening.

"Who?" Jule looks back; the guards are coming. Nearby, like an oversized slit in a mailbox, lies a hole in the floor. A black hole. She has no idea how deep it is.

The voice is coming from below.

"Come on, hurry!" A hand reaches up. Whose, she doesn't know, any more than she knows what lies down there in the impenetrable darkness beneath the glossy surface of the MegaMall. A ragged voice orders, "Hurry. Down here!"

EIGHT

THaT WaS CRaZY, SHOWING ourselves," James mutters. "We could have been caught!"

"We couldn't let them hurt that girl." No matter who the trapped girl was or what she looked like, Tick would have done the same. He'd risk everything to help any kid in that kind of trouble, but this one! She looked so brave, she looked so fiercely pretty, marching along . . . "Besides," he says, because he can't tell James any of these things, "if this works out, Security gets on the Dingos' case and kicks Burt and his mad dogs out of the mall."

"You think they won't rat on us?"

"Who's going to believe a nut case like Burt? Look. We were only on camera long enough to get their attention." Tick is trying hard to sound braver than he feels. "So what if they do know we're here? They don't know who we are or where we are."

Tick's Crazies are making their way to the new hideout by wildly different routes. He and James are running along a service corridor behind the stores, keeping low. James says what Tick is thinking. "What if they do?"

Tick turns. "It was a risk we had to take. Besides, I took precautions. For instance, the hoodies. Even if they go back and rerun their tapes, they won't know what we look like. Nobody will know it was us."

"Right," James says. "The masks."

"And Dingo colors on the flags. To make Security think it was Dingos on the balcony too. If this works out, we'll get rid of Burt and his nut jobs for good."

"It's worth it if it works."

"No. It's worth it because we saved the girl." They saved her, but where is she? Where did she go after the Dingos scattered and the guards came down? He doesn't know. Tick swallows hard.

"I guess, but still . . ."

"We've been good, we've been careful."

"What if we weren't careful enough?"

James is an old friend. His very first Castertown Crazy. They've been around here for a very long time. To make them both feel better, Tick says, "Trust me, nobody knows that the Castertown Crazies exist."

NINE

DEEP IN THE COMMAND center at the heart of the Zozzco Mega-Mall, Amos Zozz sits in solitary state, watching the goings-on as his plasma monitors bring up pictures from every sector of the MegaMall. The wall to his right is hung with masks, one gold and ceremonial-looking, one a featureless, utilitarian gray and a third in the image of Amos Zozz as he would have been if he had kept his looks. Above the bank of screens on which he watches events in his sprawling commercial empire hangs a portrait of an extremely pretty little boy with short, curly hair.

It's an oil painting, copied from a photo made at a Sears store when Amos was very young. Before everything changed. Mama Zozz, who was the underpaid housekeeper for an enormously rich family on Long Island, saved up for months to have her beautiful baby boy's photo taken by the store photographer. Dressed in a nice white shirt with a blue bow tie, handsome, manly little Amos stands in front of a blue backdrop that exactly matches his eyes.

He looks nothing like that now. Hideously disfigured by what happened to him, the rich and powerful Amos

Zozz is careful to keep out of sight. When he does meet the public, he will wear the jeweler's triumph, a handsome ceremonial mask. Meanwhile, let that daughter he had by a highly paid surrogate mother become the public face of Zozzco.

Since that awful day when he was seven, Amos has despised children, but he had to have at least one to carry on the family line. There's no point to making money if you can't keep it, and Amos will make sure Zozzco stays in the family. Where he used to pay a lawyer to conduct meetings and face the public for him, his daughter does it now. Let his idiot daughter Isabella flounce around acting important. He sighs. And to think he counted on her to produce a grandson who would make him proud.

Never mind. He has the power, and he will keep that power. Working behind the scenes the way he has all his life since that childhood trauma, Amos Zozz rules the MegaMall. Soon he will rule the commercial world, which as everybody knows really means that in time Zozzco will have control in the world of politics because everybody knows that with money, comes power. In time, he thinks, Amos Zozz will rule the entire world.

The world just doesn't know it yet.

Amos will always despise the children who made him what he is, a disfigured monster with a face that revolts everyone, but he owes those rotten little beasts a debt of thanks. Without the accident and the terrible cruelty that followed, he'd probably be just another ordinary man.

Handsome, perhaps, but without money, Amos would probably be a low-level wage slave in a business owned by some other billionaire. Unless he was unlucky enough to end up like his mother, working for heartless rich people in a mansion where she was eternally underpaid and never thanked.

If anybody gets to be rich and heartless, it's me.

It was a pair spoiled rich kids who ruined Amos for ordinary life but in the end, he owes them a big fat thank-you for making him the rich and powerful person that he is. Without the heartless Galt twins and the accident and the lawsuit that followed, Amos might be handsome and happy, but he wouldn't be rich.

The evil Galt twins lived with their beautiful, vain mother and disgustingly rich father in a mansion in Southampton, Long Island, where some of the richest people live.

Amos never had a father, at least not that he knew of, so he and Mama Zozz had to live in the basement because they were poor and Mama was only the Galt family's maid. Randy and Andy made fun of Amos all the time. They pulled his hair and they laughed at Amos when he cried, and if he told on them? Their father would have his mother fired and they would be *really* poor. Who would believe Amos? His mother was the maid. Randy and Andy called him "Amy" because of the blond curls. They tied him up and made him put on a dress. In first grade they loved to lock themselves in their beautiful playhouse in the garden and have candy and cake, and they made sure that Amos was watching through the window before they started to eat.

They wouldn't let him come in no matter how hard he begged, even though they all went to bed in the same house at night.

"You can't come in, this is our *special place*."

Then one horrible Saturday it rained. The twins got bored. Next thing Amos knew, he heard them calling, "Oh, Amy. Amy . . ."

He was so excited. They wanted him!

The playhouse door was wide open. "Come on in, we have chocolate cake."

Crash bang boom, little Amos was inside the twins' sacred playhouse, burying his face in a great big fat piece of their cake. Then the door slammed. The twins locked him inside! A window opened and something big came in on the end of a stick. It was a . . . WHAM. It slammed shut and the thing on the stick hit the floor and cracked open. It was a hornets' nest.

It was horrible. Amos screamed and hammered and cried and cried until his throat swelled up and he couldn't make another sound. He was trapped. Trapped, too small to fight off the hornets and too weak to break out of the playhouse, he felt new stings piling up on top of the first ones and there was nothing he could do.

He had lost control of his life!

By the time the gardener looked in and saw him, Amos was a knot of pain, hugging his knees as he rolled on the floor. Police had to come to get him out. They threw a gas bomb into the playhouse to kill the hornets. An ambulance came and took Amos away. He spent practically forever in the hospital, getting well. Nothing they did could make the bumps and swellings go down. The lumps stayed.

No medicine they gave him and no surgery they tried would make his hair grow back the way it was.

All Amos had left on his head were lumps and some ugly tufts. He hated Randy and Andy Galt more than anybody in the world. When he begged his mother to quit so he could go to a different school, she cried. They were poor, she told him. She begged him to understand. She needed the job!

To make up for it, Mama bought him a long blond wig. The glue hurt the lumps on his scalp but every morning Amos glued it on, and every morning the Galt twins taunted him. His face looked bad and the other kids laughed, but as long as Amos could hide behind his expensive hair, he was OK.

Until one awful day in fifth grade. Andy and Randy tackled Amos in the schoolyard. They yanked off the wig out there in front of all the other kids. The wig came off, along with the skin on his lumps and what little was left of his real hair. He could handle the pain. What still hurts to this day is the way everybody laughed. And laughed. And laughed.

Oh, he went back to school with a new wig, but it got harder and harder. Wherever he went, kids from his school, kids he didn't know, even kids from other towns made fun of him. He was bitter, but he was tough. Then one day in sixth grade, Amos went to his locker.

It looked the same but nothing was the same.

Without explanation and without warning, he was alone in the hall. Where did everybody go? *Better hurry,* he thought. *The Galts' chauffeur will be mad.* He yanked open the locker and a wasps' nest fell out, **smack!** on his head. It was terrible. Thousands poured out, stinging him relentlessly. He whirled in the storm of stinging insects and fell. He lay there helpless on the polished linoleum. Somewhere inside Amos, there was a **crack!** It wasn't his heart breaking. It was his brain.

After he healed they transferred him to a special hospital. He stayed there for a long, long time.

The Galt family paid wads of money to make Mama Zozz and Amos and all of their problems go away.

Meanwhile, in the state hospital for the mentally deranged, where he stayed after the knots of pain all over his head and body went down enough so he could move again, Amos seethed.

Children are animals. No, monsters. Children did this to him!

When the ambulance came that day and they rolled Amos out of the schoolhouse, he heard them. Heartless children like heartless witches and warlocks, cackling. Amos Zozz rolled out of the schoolhouse flailing and helpless for the last time in his life. For the last time in his life, he heard them laughing at him.

Well, he'll show *them*.

Brooding over his banks of monitors, tracking them through his MegaMall, Amos Zozz still hears their laughter. It won't stop until he does what he has to, and gets what he wants. Revenge.

And when he does, when he has them all trapped and begging for mercy, then it will be his turn to laugh.

In the state mental hospital, waiting for his lumps to go down so he could pretend to smile and convince them he was cured, Amos made three vows.

I will take control of my life and I will never lose it again.

On the typewriter in the hospital dayroom, Amos

made a list of instructions for his mother. He wrote all the letters, but Mama made the calls. The lawyer they hired thought he was working for Mama Zozz, not a twelve-year-old boy. They sued the Galts for damages and in the end, Amos took half of everything they had. He bought a little house where he lived with Mama Zozz until she died. The rest of the money, he banked. He taught himself about the stock market and began buying and selling stocks and bonds.

He never went back to school.

And his second vow? *I will rule the world.*

He's working on it! Over the years, the old man has watched his millions make more millions. He is worth several billion, billion dollars now.

That leaves the third. *The children will suffer for what they did to me.* All children. *I'll make them pay.*

And soon, he thinks, watching Dingos scurrying like ants on one of his video screens. Alone in the empty room, the old man feels his pale, lumpy face ripping wide open. It is an unfamiliar sensation. The last time he felt it was when he read in the newspapers that the evil Galt twins had gone bankrupt.

Now his raw face is ripping open that same way.

Only his mother would know that Amos is smiling.

He is close to carrying out his diabolical scheme.

A voice comes crackling into the room, interrupting his reverie. The face of his chief of Security pops up on every screen. "There are children in the mall, Sir. Wild children." He is angry and puffing. Rattling the doorknob outside the booth. "We almost caught one."

Amos has a choice here: put on one of the masks he wears to meet the public, or do what he does. "I told you never to bother me here."

"This is urgent. Let me in."

"If it's that urgent, you can file a report. Now, go."

"But Sir! There are KIDS infesting the MegaMall." The Security chief is outraged. "My men saw them. They're running like rats in the galleries. Dozens of them."

"No," Amos says. "Hundreds."

"Trashing and pillaging, we have to . . . What?"

"No." If he allowed anybody but family inside this office, the chief of Security would see Amos wringing his hands like a mantis studying its prey. "More."

"Sir!"

He's not sure how many, he only knows that feral children have filtered into several widely separated sectors of his MegaMall and he has been watching them. Oh, he's been watching them. The place is so big that as far as he knows, none of them know who the others are. Well, he thinks, soon enough the whole world will know. "Maybe thousands."

"Sir, you're not hearing me. The place is overrun by *children*. They're running wild and we have to . . ."

Coldly, Amos says, "I know."

"Well, what do you want me to do?"

"Nothing, until I give the word."

On the screen, his Security chief's face is like a pink balloon getting bigger and bigger. "But," he blusters. "But . . ."

Tenting his fingers, Amos sits back. "Nothing."

His angry chief is too angry to recognize his tone. "But they'll ruin everything! I can't just let them . . ."

The old man's voice turns to steel as he says ominously, "Do as I say. Understand." Amos pauses, weighting every word of the threat that follows like a lead sinker. "You wouldn't be the first Security chief I've fired."

TEN

Mag cries, "They almost got us!"

Loyal to the end, Tidgewell says, "It's that guy Tick Stiles's fault."

"Stiles and his stupid Crazies." Barlow punches the wall.

"I'll get you. I. Will. Get. You," Burt Arno spits, but he isn't so sure.

Around him, his ragtag Dingos repeat, "Get you. Yeah!" With their black headbands and stripes of black paint on their pale, pearly faces, Burt Arno's tribe is a shabby, disgruntled mess.

Shaken by their brush with Security, the Dingos have regrouped at their hideout in an abandoned back alley that connects the Romanesque Sector to the amusement plaza. One minute they were on the march with their captive in tow and the next, they had guards thundering down on them. All right, they were squealing like scared pigs when they scattered and fled. Embarrassing? Yes. This is the worst.

More than anything he can think of, getting embarrassed

makes Burt Arno roaring, tearing mad. He is also confused. Frustrated, because he thought he had a plan.

And the girl they caught in Dingo territory?

Disappeared. Totally gone.

There is no finding her now.

"Rotten Crazies." Burt spits out a string of threats. "I'm going to get you crummy . . ."

His messy minions echo. "Crummy . . ."

". . . Scummy . . ."

"Scummy . . ."

"Stupid Castertown Crazies," Burt explodes. "Bringing down Security on us Dingos," he rages. "Well, curse you all."

Everybody goes, "Curse you all!"

"I will hunt you down . . ."

The Dingos mutter, "Hunt you down . . ."

"And I will find you . . ."

"Find you . . ." They are still panting from the chase. Two dozen rough boys and one tough redheaded girl squat in a grim little circle around their leader, waiting.

After considerable thought Burt says, "And when I do . . ."

"And when he does . . ." Warlike in shredded denim and studded jackets and T-shirts with the names of defunct rock bands picked out in glitter, the Dingos wait for Burt to complete the plan.

Burt is beyond speech.

The Dingos have never seen him madder. In spite of the chase and the humiliation, in spite of having to hide in the garbage behind the Grecian Food Court, holding their noses while Security tramped past, the Dingos have made it safely back to the lair. They are Burt Arno's people. They have been his people ever since they got in trouble at school back in Castertown and the Town Council put them away in the State Orphans' Home.

Burt's not a bad guy, he just needs a good gang around him to make him feel strong. As long as he has the toughest gang in the territory, he's OK.

He collected this gang in the State Home, where he founded the Dingo Tribe. In the State Home, they ruled. Then Burt broke them out and brought them here to the MegaMall, and it all changed. He didn't know how to get around. Stiles did, and Burt hates him for it.

A kid with a gang to protect knows you have to get in good with the Man, whoever that is, right? In this place, it's Amos Zozz. Nobody's ever seen him but everybody's afraid of him; Burt knows. And to get friends with the power, you bring them a present, right? Like, a great big Sacrifice. He had the idea that delivering that girl Jule to the Dark Hall would somehow get him in good with Amos Zozz, and when it did? Watch out, Tick Stiles.

Burt's new best friend Amos would drive out the Castertown Crazies, and Burt and his Dingos would rule the MegaMall.

He'd . . .

Well, look how that turned out.

Instead of getting in good with the man in charge, he has crossed the powerful Amos Zozz. He can't let on to the Dingos, but he's scared. Burt is their main man, but right now, Burt is not exactly himself.

He and his Dingos are holed up in the shell of an abandoned souvenir store, sitting in the nest of grimy quilts and rugs and stained bedding that passes for home. Burt has been silent for too long. The Dingos shift on their haunches, waiting for him to make the next threat.

They're getting anxious and Burt knows it. He blusters, "I. Will. Make. You. Pay."

Two dozen Dingos let out their breath at once. "How?"

He spins, considering. When nothing comes, he blurts: "Revenge!"

Only Kirk can get away with asking the next question. Burt's second in command says, "OK, what kind of revenge?"

"I just told you," Burt says weakly. "Terrible revenge." The truth is, he doesn't know

But the Dingos are staring. *Burt, where did you just go in your head?* He growls, "Revenge!"

"Like . . ." Puzzled, Kirk repeats. "Like what?"

"Don't ask!" He can forget about Amos. That mess with Security just blew that plan away. It's kids against grownups in this tremendous, scary place and right now Burt needs all the help he can get, just to survive. The rock-bottom truth is that Burt's been hanging in here in the Romanesque Sector instead of moving on not because he wants to take over, but because he doesn't know what to do. He needs Tick Stiles.

Burt would never admit it but Tick's smarter than he, and he can't go far until he knows at least half of what Tick knows about getting around and staying safe. Burt Arno needs to get friends with the guy so he'll help them, but he can't let on. He has to keep his people together so he roars, "Horrible revenge!"

Barlow and Tidgewell raise their fists, shouting like Burt, "Awful revenge!"

Two dozen Dingos raise their fists. "Bloody revenge."

"Revenge," redheaded Mag Sullivan bellows, louder than the rest. Mag, who lost their captive, thinks maybe if she yells loud enough, they'll forget. She jogs Burt's elbow. Like, she's pushing him into something he isn't ready to do. "Right, Burt?"

Like— *that,* Burt wheels on her. Her best friend— no, her only friend here lashes out: "It's all your fault!"

"It wasn't me, it . . ." It isn't fair! One minute she had the prisoner, she did! Mag gripped that girl so hard that her fingers froze, with the right ones clamped on her shoulder and the left knotted in her hair. The next, she was empty-handed. The girl from town was gone and Mag was on the run.

"You're the one who let go!" Kirk jabs his finger into her. "Admit it. It was you."

Barlow and Tidgewell wheel, pointing at Mag. "You let her go."

"Burt, tell them it wasn't my . . ."

"It was so your fault," Burt says, because he has to blame somebody for the mess they're in. "Now you have to pay."

It is like a slap in the face.

Kirk rakes her with a mean grin. ". . . have to pay."

Barlow and Tidgewell repeat on the same note, ". . . to pay."

"Pay," the Dingos mutter, and the echo goes around the circle. ". . . pay."

The silence that follows is awful. They are all staring.

"OK," Mag says. "If you want to hit me or something, get it over with."

"After the sit-down," Burt says.

"But I don't need a . . ."

"Sit-down." Barlow shoves her off balance.

"I don't want . . ."

"Sit-down!" Tidgewell shoves from the other side.

"Sit-down." The surly group buzzes like a bunch of wasps.

Mag's heart goes thudding into her socks. "Please don't. Let go!"

Kirk wrestles her into the center of the circle. "Think fast, girl. What are you going to say?"

When a Dingo messes up, Burt Arno calls a sit-down. It isn't a trial, exactly, but it is. Whatever went wrong, that person gets exactly three sentences to explain. Then Burt calls for a vote and no matter what the facts are, his Dingos vote to kick that person out of the tribe. Mag doesn't know what this means, exactly, as in, what happens to that person after Burt takes away the jacket and strips off the headband, but she knows it's bad. Once a Dingo gets kicked out of the tribe, you never see that Dingo again.

What am I going to say? she wonders, thinking fast. *What would I do if they kicked me out? Where would I go?* For as long as she's lived here in the MegaMall, Mag has eaten and slept and run with the Dingos. Before she came here Mag Sullivan lived with a whole string of foster parents. The last ones were so bad that she ran away. Burt found her sobbing in the State Home where the cops had dumped her, and she's been a Dingo ever since. For Mag Sullivan, this is the best home she's ever had. Face it, it's the only home, but now . . .

Burt is saying, "Let's hear it, Mag. Three sentences."

She can't find even one!

I didn't do it won't cut it. She has to explain!

Burt says, "So?"

Two dozen Dingos hiss. "So?"

Perched on a crate in the center of the circle, Mag can't figure out what to say. *Look, Burt. What was I supposed to do?* No good, Mag. Think again.

They were OK until the Castertown Crazies popped up on the balcony with their nutty little display. And then Stiles and his gang of lost kids had the nerve to disappear!

Naturally Security forces swarmed down on the Dingos instead. They came on in formation, swinging nets and chains. In all Mag's life in the MegaMall, it was the scariest thing she's ever seen. They were coming down on her with raised bats and studded maces, and the sinister end men were swinging weighted nets that could bring you down if they hooked your feet or settled over your head. One wrong move and Mag would have been the prisoner, not that girl. She thinks, *Who wouldn't drop everything and run? Besides,* she thinks, *that girl wasn't doing anything to us, not really.*

She's afraid to tell Burt what she is thinking: *You're just scared she'll turn you in.*

There. Three sentences. The wrong ones. She covers her mouth.

Burt says, "Are you going to talk or what?"

This is awful. She can't. No, she won't.

"Well?" Burt stands.

Mag stands.

"What? What!" Burt's face is like a clenched fist. They are standing toe to toe. Tough, redheaded Mag Sullivan and Burt Arno face off. He glowers. "What do you have to say?"

Think, Mag Sullivan. Think fast. She says, low, so the others won't hear, "I thought you were my friend."

And just like that, Burt throws their friendship out the window, bellowing, "After what you did?"

Mag says carefully, "Your friend is your friend no matter what, Burt." She is coming to a decision here.

But Burt is too angry to see that Mag Sullivan is changing. "Not today, Mag. We lost our prisoner. Somebody has to pay."

Speechless, she shrugs.

Burt chokes. "If nothing else, apologize!"

As one the tribe turns— not accusing, exactly, but waiting. The word hangs in the air between them.

Apologize.

This is bad. They are waiting for her to grovel.

What she says next surprises even Mag. "Never," she says defiantly. Younger than he is, beholden to him, really, she defies Burt Arno. Just like that.

Burt is silent for much too long. Then his eyes rip across her face like twin lasers. "*What* did you say?"

Mag won't bother to answer. Turning, she nudges aside several of the smallest, scruffiest Dingos with her toe and threads her way out of the circle. Before Burt even guesses that she is turning her back on him, probably forever, Mag Sullivan walks out of the Dingo tribe.

"Wait!" Burt roars after her. "What did you say?"

Pausing at the exit, she coughs up the words like a hairball. "I said, goodbye."

Then she runs.

ELEVEN

WHEN THE TROUBLE STARTED Tick saw the girl jerk free of her captors; she ran with her head high and her hair flying. From his hiding place on the balcony, he saw that brave girl duck and roll behind a trash barrel. Before he could think of a way to save her she disappeared. Where is she now?

He only saw her for a minute, but he can't get her out of his head.

He should have jumped down and grabbed her, but he couldn't blow his cover. He had to wait until Security chased the Dingos into the courtyard and around the fountain and on to the next sector, where great glass sliding doors whooshed open and then shut, sealing off the Dingos' squeals and the thunder of the guards' footsteps and their angry shouts.

Then he had to see to his Crazies; it's his job to keep them safe. At Tick's signal the night children melted away, as planned. They fanned out in twos and threes, with each group taking a different route to the new hideout. Tick's people left so quickly and silently that it took him a minute to realize they were gone.

Running along the service corridor with James, he weighed it: his people's safety. The girl. His Crazies have been together for so long that they know the drill. The bigs will take care of the littles, using the maps Tick copied for them and handed out before they started this. They are, after all, Tick's people. He can count on them to follow the plan. He knows they'll find their way to the new place without being seen. They will filter into the music gallery and enter the new hideout, no problem. By the time Tick gets back they'll be settled in, with bedrolls laid out and supplies safely stashed. He'll find them sitting around over their last meal before the mall lights come up on the new business day and they have to go to bed.

OK then.

He turned back so fast just now that James ran up his heels. "What?"

"I have to go back."

"That's crazy!"

"Find Willie, get the kids settled. I'll be there as soon as I can."

He is back in the deserted gallery, looking for the girl. It shouldn't be his problem, really, but Tick is worried about her. Alone, she won't last five minutes in the Mega-Mall. Either Security will bring her down or she'll run into something worse.

Unlike his night children, this fiery girl with the fly-away hair is new to the life. She doesn't know how to live in this place. Who's going to warn her to crouch and freeze when a surveill camera swings around, or tell her where they are placed? There are hundreds of hidden cameras. They feed multiple screens in Security booths in every sector, Tick knows. What if they spot her and a squad comes crashing out? Will she know where to hide? There are too many unknown corridors in the MegaMall, too many blind passages with no exits and too many false trails; she could run for days and still get caught.

There are worse things to watch out for— the nightly disinfectant spray, or the whirling brushes and powerful vacuum hoses of the cleaning machines that roll through the corridors at odd hours. Walking free is a problem even for old-timers like Tick. She needs somebody to show her how.

This is what Tick Stiles does best. He takes good care of people, which is why his little tribe moves like a sweet machine.

Alone in the gallery, he stands, listening. It should be simple work to find her but the glistening corridor is completely still. "It's OK, you can come out now." His whisper echoes. No one answers.

Cautiously, he advances on the overturned trash barrel, left behind by heedless Security troops. "Are you there?"

Nothing.

He takes a long look down the glistening expanse of marble. Nobody around but Tick. Impatient, he stalks the corridor, scoping the balconies above. Nothing moves. There is nothing stirring in the sunken rest areas with their potted plants and curved stone benches and there is nobody skulking in the shadow of the long balcony. There's just Tick, standing in the middle of the empty corridor looking this way, then that.

First he saw her. Now he doesn't.

In the deserted gallery with every storefront shuttered there aren't many places to hide, so where is she?

Gone.

In that tone he uses when he wants to be heard without alerting Security, Tick calls. "Girl?"

He thinks he sees something moving but it's only a forgotten Easter display in a toy store window, a giant inflated bunny wagging back and forth behind the metal grille.

He tries, "Don't be scared."

No answer. Poor kid, alone in the night. She needs his help, but how can he help if he can't find her?

He doesn't know. "It's OK, really. I'm here."

Tick catches a slight movement out of the corner of his eye. It's a bank of artificial ferns rattling in a blast of central air.

"Girl?"

The silence is intense.

In the next second the floor shivers. All the hairs on the back of his neck stand up. *What?*

Beneath his feet, the vibration grows until the floor shudders. It's like standing on the back of a sleeping beast. *What!* In seconds it subsides. Oh. He relaxes. Something in the underground service tunnels that mirror the corridors of the giant honeycomb. Night tram.

Tick says softly, "I'm not going to hurt you, OK?"

Depending on what this girl wants, he'll either help her phone home or keep her safe until morning when her folks come looking for her. If she wants, he can lead her to the nearest transport bay so the morning cleanup crews will find her when they come in. It'd probably be safer to keep her in the new hideout until 10 a.m. when the shoppers come flooding in, but first he has to convince her to come.

After tangling with the Dingos, would you go with the first kid who asked?

"Look," he says patiently. "I'm going to sit down on the floor and count to ten or something. OK, I won't count, I'll just close my eyes and if you want to come out or anything, you can come out. OK?"

Dangerous as it is in this place where you never know who's watching or what's coming, Tick Stiles folds up, tailor fashion, and sits on the floor with his hands resting on his knees. He turns up his palms to make clear to this girl, if she is watching, that even if she shows herself he isn't about to pounce. He's just going to sit here with his hands open and if she wants to come out and come close enough to talk to him, she can do it. She can see from the way he is sitting right now that he isn't about to get up and chase her. He won't do anything to frighten her, he'll just sit, waiting for as long as it takes.

He is so still that it's almost like not breathing. Everything about Tick advertises the fact that he's no threat. He could sit forever if he had to if this was an ordinary mall but it isn't; in the MegaMall, you're always in danger of getting caught. He can at least sit here long enough for the girl to get over her fear and show herself.

As it turns out, he can't.

He hears a sound: feet drumming.

It's Security, coming back.

"OK," he says. "If you're coming out, you should do it fast."

He hears them pounding down the far corridor into the Grecian courtyard. Soon they will be here.

"I can't wait much longer."

He should go, but he lingers. Quiet as a hermit squatting in the desert, Tick waits. He hears the squad thud-thudding around the fountain and out of the courtyard into the gallery where he is sitting, but he waits. Tick has lived here long enough to know how to vanish before they reach him. The guards are coming closer. Still he waits.

Then somebody shouts, "Mall rat!"

The guards break formation and charge.

"Girl," Tick says in a whisper that carries farther than any shout, "if you want me to help you, it's gotta be now."

The guards' boot heels clatter like rocks on a tin roof. In another minute they'll be on top of him — and still no sign of the girl.

"Girl," he says desperately. "Please!"

Tick waits until he's waited too long.

"Girl?"

Another minute and they'll have him.

"Hey," Tick hisses, darting into the shadows, "if you aren't coming, hide!"

TWELVE

WHO ARE YOU?" TERRIFIED, Jule is gasping. She can't catch her breath. Her plunge into the darkness was that swift.

Minutes ago she was sprawled on the marble. Roaring down on her in their black helmets, MegaMall Security looked like a platoon of tremendous bugs.

Now she is here.

Wherever this is.

Underground.

She and the tall stranger who pulled her down the hatch into the tunnel are rushing along in the dark. The light tram she is riding in speeds along a track lit at ground level by orange bulbs not much brighter than fireflies. The halogen headlight bores a small hole in the darkness ahead but she can barely see the boy sitting in front of her. They zoom past the gaping mouths of other tunnels, past loading zones and past red exit lights, with no sign of stopping. They are in the belly of the MegaMall.

Jule Devereaux and her unknown rescuer sit in the little cockpit like passengers on a bullet train. All she can see of him is the back of his head.

"Where are we going?"

All she gets back is the lonely whir of the wheels.

"So, um. You can't talk, or don't want to?"

He shrugs.

"A word would be nice."

If only he'd turn and *look* at her.

"You don't have to talk, OK? Just nod your head."

They ride along in silence.

At least she's escaped Security. Anything's better than being snared in those weighted nets and dragged to head-quarters. Grownups tell you the Zozzco guards are there to protect you, but nobody knows for sure. What they do remains secret, specific to the MegaMall.

In fact, everything is specific to the MegaMall. Nobody from Castertown works here after the last shop closes and the last cleanup crew gets on the shuttle to the parking lot. From 11 p.m. to 8 a.m. the mall belongs to Security. Everybody wonders, but nobody knows. Kids tell tales: If the guards catch you, first they shave your head. Then they paint you with Magic Marker and throw you out with the trash. No, they lock you up and keep you until you're too old to walk. Or they stick you in the stockroom and make you stack crates and unpack cartons for the rest of your life.

Unless you end up in the State Home.

So when the mysterious hand popped out of the floor just minutes ago, she dropped into the hole, like that! The steel grate closed over their heads with the finality of a lid. She had no choice! He led her down a steep ladder. Whoever he is. Now she is riding along behind a strange, big guy who won't talk to her. She should be frightened, but for the moment, she's relieved.

There's something steady about him. Even the silence is reassuring. He doesn't have to tell her this is a rescue: the grate, the hidden entrance, the waiting car. It was all quick and smooth— as though he's done this or something like it a dozen times before.

"So, OK," she says briskly. "Where to?"

He won't answer her— she already knows. He hasn't spoken since he reached out and pulled her in, but Jule is impatient. Feisty. She's not the kind of person who gives up.

"So, are you going to talk to me or what?"

He pushes a lever and the little car veers into a side passage, hugging the track.

Frustrated, Jule taps him on the shoulder to get his attention. He shakes her off. "Well, if you aren't going to talk, the least you can do is look at me!"

He shrugs as if to acknowledge that he's heard her, but does not turn.

"Or growl. Or *something*," she says crossly. "Come on!"

He doesn't even snort. So much for conversation, Jule thinks. The silence is getting on her nerves.

With a screech the car whips around a curve and rolls on, into a new sector. She has no idea where they're going. All she knows is that they're on a track somewhere underneath the giant mall.

After a time she tries again. "If you won't look at me, you can at least tell me where we are."

Her rescuer, if that's what he is, goes on as if she hasn't even spoken. He keeps his eyes on the track, intent on whatever is ahead.

She tries to keep her voice steady but it comes out on

an ascending note. "So, is this a service tunnel or what? Answer!"

As if.

Escaping the guards is a good thing, she supposes, but who is this big guy in the camouflage jacket, and why won't he talk to her? They round a curve so sharp that their necks snap. Yet another sector, she supposes, but he won't talk to her and there's no way of knowing until he does.

"This is stupid," she says finally. "Come on. Explain!"

He speaks so abruptly that she jumps. "Shut up. We're almost there."

They aren't, as it turns out, at least she thinks they aren't. The car rolls on without slowing. She says, "So, thanks for saving me . . ."

To her surprise he says, without turning, "No big."

Metal grinds on metal as the little car slows down. ". . . I guess."

The boy's big shoulders shift as he digs into a pocket. He comes up with a silver tube and hands it over his shoulder.

"What's this?"

"Just take it."

It is a PowerBar. With her mouth watering, Jule tears off the Mylar with her teeth. "Thanks! I didn't know I was so . . ."

"Shh."

"Hungry."

"Shh!"

Strange, big guy, won't talk, won't look at her. Nice, she thinks— the PowerBar— but she can't be sure. If only it was a little lighter down here. If only she could get a good look at him.

This is taking too long.

They are rolling along an unbroken stretch of track now— no curves, no tunnel mouths yawning on either side, no loading docks or exits in sight. The darkness and silence are getting to her.

"I'm Jule Devereaux, in case you want to know." Jule starts off sounding strong and tough. After too long she adds, "From Castertown?"

The silence is awful.

"Are you going to tell me your name or anything?"

"No."

"At least turn around and look at me."

He has a deep voice. "Too dark."

Jule doesn't mean to quaver, but this is all too much. She says in an anxious little squeak, "Do it anyway?"

"Don't," he says. "Don't go all weird on me."

"Then act like I'm really here," she snaps.

He shrugs. "Whatever." As if he's doing her a huge favor, the strange boy turns in his seat.

In spite of herself, Jule shrieks. Who wouldn't? His face is covered by a black ski mask.

"Shhh!"

"The mask!"

"Don't scream like that."

"Why not?"

His voice drops to a pebbly whisper. "You'll wake them up!"

"Who?"

"Never mind."

Jule says, louder, "I asked you, who?"

"Shut up," he hisses, "you'll bring them down on us."

"Then take off the mask!"

"Mask? Oh, right." He pulls it off. In the darkness she can't make out his face, not really; he looks almost grown, but the bushy white hair stands up like a little boy's. He says bashfully, "I forgot."

"That's better," Jule says. "Now, what's your name?"

"It's not important." He hits a button and the car jerks to a stop. He slaps her door open and points. "This is where you get out."

"Wait!"

"Go." Leaning over the back of his seat, he puts a hand on her shoulder and pushes her out.

She is standing on a little platform. "Wait a minute!"

He slams the car door behind her.

"Aren't you coming?"

"No. Just look for the ladder. You'll come up in a music store."

"But who . . ."

"Don't worry, you'll be all right."

"Wait a minute . . ."

"Just ask for Tick." Then Lance the Loner hits the lever and the car whirs off, leaving her in the dark.

Wait.

THIRTEEN

JUST WHEN HE THINKS they are safe, just when Tick thinks nobody will ever find them here in the Music Sector, there is a disturbance in the back of the abandoned store. "What!" he shouts, whirling. "What!"

The girl he saved and spent half the night looking for blunders out of the back room, blinking. "Where am I?"

All that time lost looking, and now, just when he has his Crazies settled and least needs another distraction, here she is. He's so mad at himself for being glad to see her that he smacks her on the shoulder, hard. "How did you get in?"

They are both at the end of a long, tough night. Crossly, she shrugs him off. "What's it to you?"

"Where were you?"

"Who are you, anyway?"

"Where were you all this time?"

Turning, she takes in the scene in the abandoned music store. "What is this place?"

"Never mind." It's dawn and Tick needs to get the hideout sealed before the morning cleaning crews roll into the music gallery. His Crazies have taped the cracks in the false front so their lights won't show. They nailed rugs over the wooden door to the outside so people can talk and move around in here without being heard. Now, just as Tick thinks their hideout is secured; just when he thinks he has it sealed so tight that nobody can find them, this new girl simply wanders in with her hair flying and that fierce, wild glare. She's standing there as if she owns the place. He can't say, *I was so worried.* Instead, he attacks. "How did you get in?"

Distracted, the Crazies drop what they are doing and stare.

"What are you looking at? Get back to work!"

There is a stir as the Castertown Crazies turn and pretend to keep on doing what they were doing.

"Girl, I asked you a question! How did you get in?"

"I just did." She isn't giving an inch. "What's your problem?"

"If you can get in, anybody can get in! Were you followed?"

They are close to having a fight. "How am I supposed to know?"

The long night is getting to Tick and he can't control the anger in his tone. "Where were you when I was looking for you?"

"To, what, hand me back to that gang?"

"I was trying to *help* you."

"Fine." She wheels. "I have to go."

He grabs her wrist. "Wait! It isn't safe."

"Don't!"

"You can't go out there. Not now." This is going very badly. Tick tightens his grip.

"Why not?" Angry, she tries to pry off his fingers.

"Stop that. Look. If you want to get along here, you have to be careful and be quiet."

"What?"

"You heard me. You can't rush out, it isn't safe. You have to wait. Think. You have to be cool."

The girl stands there, considering. "OK," she says at last. "OK."

Tick lets her go. "OK," he says. "Let's start over. What are you doing here?"

"It's not like I wanted to come. Some strange, big guy dumped me in the tunnel. He said ask for Tick." Then she stops. "Wait. Are you him?"

Oh, Tick thinks. *Oh.* Surprised, he grins. "Maybe."

"I heard voices up here and I . . . Why are you smiling?"

"Never mind. The kid that dropped you. White hair, ski mask?"

"How did you know?" Now she is smiling too.

"Old friend, sort of."

"He wasn't very friendly. Won't talk to you, never smiles, doesn't look you in the face."

"That would be Lance the Loner. We don't hang out, but he's a friend."

"He lives down there?"

Tick says, "I don't know where he lives."

"It's dark in those tunnels. Creepy."

"You were about to get in worse trouble," Tick says.

"You mean the guards."

"No. The Dingos. They were marching you off to do . . . I don't know what, but it looked bad."

"Oh!" Her voice changes. "I get it now. That was you with the flags and the noise and the plastic."

"Pretty much."

"You!" The sweep of her hand takes in everybody in the room: James and Willie stacking supplies while the littles fold up their banners and deflated wading ponds and Jiggy and Nance lay out food like old troupers— the Castertown Crazies. Minus one, although Tick does not yet know that one of his kids is missing. "You're the guys who brought out the guards!"

This makes his grin even broader. "Yeah."

"Well, thanks . . . I guess." The girl screws up her face the way you do at the doctor's, when you're about to get a shot. "Look, I really have to go."

Tick is too smart to warn her all over again. Instead he asks, "You want to go home?"

"Yes. No. I don't know, exactly. Everybody's gone." There is a long, long pause while she considers. "But I can't stay here."

"If you leave now, you'll end up in the State Home. That's where Security sends lost kids. You have to wait."

She says in a low voice, "I can't."

"You have to. Go out in the morning, when you can blend in. You know, at high tide."

"Right. When gazillion shoppers are here."

"Yep. Noon's best. People don't see you, they're all about their lunch." Tick grins. Good. "Look, if you want to call your mom or your dad, we have the store phone."

She doesn't answer right away. When she does it comes as a surprise. "I don't exactly have a mom and dad," she says. "No. Wait."

"What?"

"I do, but I don't know where they are." She is deciding whether to tell him. "They. Ah. They kind of disappeared."

"Disappeared!" Tick's eyes snap wide. "What happened?"

"I don't know." The look that crosses her pretty face is stuck somewhere between grief and confusion. She's trying to explain something she doesn't understand. Finally she tells him, "I was in bed. People came. I heard them arguing. When I woke up they were gone."

Tick says carefully, "When?"

"What?"

"When did it happen?"

"Before the Grand Opening, I think."

"I'm sorry." This is all Tick says, but certain pieces are coming together in his head.

"I was little. It's been years." She's trying to smile but it isn't exactly working. "It's OK. I live with Aunt Christy."

Right, Tick thinks. *And I live here.* He offers, "So do you want to call your aunt or what?"

She corrects. "Or I did. I haven't seen her since Sunday."

"Like, she took off?"

Her voice drops. "Unless they took her."

This has so many echoes for Tick that he can't get past it. "Didn't you call the cops?"

Her face goes eight different ways. "And end up in the State Home?"

Tick grimaces. "I thought that was only for kids they catch here."

"Like you." She looks at him with clear gray eyes.

Something passes between them. He nods. "Like me."

"No," she says. "They pick up any kid who's lost their family anywhere, and dump them in the Home."

His voice sinks. It isn't a question. "And nobody asks where their families went."

"No." Tick won't know it, but Jule Devereaux is repeating Aunt Christy the day her folks vanished. She is saying exactly what Aunt Christy said, in that same flat tone of despair, "You can't even trust the police. It isn't safe in Castertown."

"That's terrible."

The girl looks into her hands the way you do when you don't want people to see what you are thinking. "It's . . . Agh."

"I know." Tick doesn't know her well enough to tell her what happened to him, at least not yet. He says kindly, "You don't look so good."

"It's nothing!" Her pretty face is a mess but she tries to pass it off with, "Probably I'm just hungry."

"When was the last time you ate?"

"I don't know. Yesterday lunch, I guess." Then she blushes. "Oh, right. PowerBar. This guy Lance gave me a PowerBar."

"Right. Lance the Loner."

"I was so hungry I forgot I was eating." This sounds so stupid that Tick laughs and the girl laughs.

The Crazies take this as a signal that everything's OK, and drop what they're doing to gather around.

"I'm Tick Stiles."

"Right."

"I kind of . . ."

"Run this place," she finishes as the Crazies drift into the circle. "Hi. I'm Jule Devereaux."

"And these are my main men Willie and James," Tick says. "The purple hair's Jiggy and that's Nance . . . Don't worry, there won't be a names quiz. These guys—" He waves toward the rest and as he does so realizes they're one short, no time to deal with that now, just finish the introductions and get everybody settled before the morning cleaning shift rolls in. "These are the Castertown Crazies."

"Nice to meet you."

Then, because the hideout is shipshape and James is nuking a carton of Belgian waffles that fell off a truck in the wide service corridor that runs behind all the stores, Tick grabs two paper plates and offers her one. He points to narrow steps leading to an abandoned platform. "Sit down. Eat."

IT IS LATER. THE other Crazies have laid out their bedrolls and crawled in to sleep but Jule and Tick are still talking. In the stillness, she turns to him. "You never said what you're doing here."

"Who, me? What does it look like?"

"Hiding out, I guess, but why?"

"No place to go," he says.

"You too?"

"Nobody home," he says. "I don't even know if home's there any more."

"That's terrible."

"Not really, the mall's OK. Enough to eat and there's always plenty to do." After all these years the next thing still sticks like a rock in his throat. Tick coughs. "Besides, my folks are gone."

"Gone!"

"Disappeared, pretty much."

"Oh." A shiver goes through her. "Like mine."

He nods.

But she won't leave it at that. When he doesn't go on she says, "So, what? Did you wake up one morning and they were gone?"

"Not exactly. It happened here. I was on one of the rides and when I got off they weren't anywhere."

"This is too weird," Jule says.

"What do you mean?"

"I don't know yet." In this light the girl's eyes are almost too clear. As if he can see straight through to the back of her head. "When did you lose them?"

He shrugs. "For all I know, they lost me. You don't always know whose fault it is."

"Unless you do. Now, when did it happen?"

"Don't get hung up on this, but . . . Agh." Tick doesn't know why it's so hard to get out the rest, but it is. "It was the day before the Grand Opening."

Jule's face tightens. She is squinting at something he can't see. "Did they, um, work for Zozzco?"

"They were the architects."

"Wow!"

"What do you mean, wow?"

"Oh, wow. Mine designed the WhirlyFunRide." For the

first time since she blundered in here Jule's whole face lights up. She elbows him. "Don't you think that's strange?"

"Everything's strange," Tick says, but before he can follow up he hears frantic hammering.

Just when they most need to be quiet, there is someone banging on the wooden false front of the abandoned music store. At the sound, Willie and James get up, ready to fight off whatever comes. Waving them away, Tick darts into the crawl space between the glass store window and the protective wall.

"Shut up!" he hisses.

The knocking doesn't stop. "Hurry!"

"Who is it?"

A little voice flutes, "Hurry up, it's me!"

Hissing for silence, Willie and James tug at the carpet covering the outside door they spent so much time securing.

"Come on, let me in!"

"Shut up, we're coming!" Tick takes his knife and pulls out the staples. Together the three boys pull back a flap just wide enough for whoever it is to stop hammering and come in, for Pete's sake.

"Doakie!"

Instead a fuzzy, gangly black dog scrambles in, yapping wildly in spite of the fact that behind it, somebody is going, "Shh shh, shut up, Puppy! Puppy, shut up!"

It is a half-grown Scottie from a pet store.

Next Doakie wriggles through the hole.

Tick groans. "Don't you know we can't keep pets in here?"

"Oh please," Doakie wails. "He got too big to sell!"

"If he barks they'll all come down on us!"

"They left him tied up out back," Doakie says, and what he says next is both mystifying and terrible, "and the truck was coming to take him to the Dark Hall!"

FOURTEEN

IT IS a week later.

Burt Arno is in a tearing hurry. It's been seven days since he lost his living sacrifice. Excuse me. The girl he was delivering to the Dark Hall for personal reasons.

OK, he thought it would get him in good with old man Zozz, who could care less if he lives or dies. Less, he supposes, since his one big chance to get tight with the man in power went up in smoke. If Amos Zozz was watching from on high or something, he saw what a frooging failure Burt is, and if he knows, and it made him mad . . .

Yikes, he thinks. *What if he wants me to die?*

Burt has reason to worry. Seven days since the disaster, and with every one of them, things are getting worse.

It took him 'til now to track Stiles and his band of geeky sub-teens and half-baked rug rats to their new hideout. Hurrying along, Burt is itching for a confrontation. If he's ever going to be top dog here, he has to hit Stiles so hard that he flies out of the ballpark. Where Burt comes from, that's the way it's done. *Gangs rule,* he thinks. *I rule.* He hopes.

He thuds along thinking, *Just wait'll they get a load of this*. He is carrying a hastily lettered note.

> Wynton Marsalis fountain at 4 a.m.
> Be there or be dead. Come alone.
> Burt Arno

Good, he thinks, rereading. This is really good. Plus, it's written in blood. This time, he'll do like I say. Nice touch, Burt cut himself shaving, so there you go. See, he and his Dingos ran away from the State Home so long ago that Barlow and Tidgewell have faint moustaches, and once a week Burt and his best buddy Kirk scrape their faces with six-track razors to get rid of the fuzz.

Tonight his hand slipped. Maybe he's a little bit nervous about this meeting. Partly, he doesn't know what he'll do or say. Get revenge on the Crazies, he supposes. Get the girl back, so he can offer her up to the real ruler of this place. Or is he getting cranked up to beg for help?

He doesn't know. He doesn't know!

Truth is, with Mag gone, Burt doesn't know what he wants.

With her gone, he doesn't know where to start.

He doesn't even know what to say.

Um. "Hand over my sacrifice?"

Now, what Burt means by "sacrifice" is a puzzle to him. He just knows that there is a Dark Hall, that Amos Zozz is the ruler and if he could just get friends with him, everything would be fine. Last week he thought he'd found just the thing to do the trick, after which at Zozzco, he'd be a VIP. The old man would thank Burt for the present, and Burt would have him in his power. This Amos would do whatever Burt said, like throw Stiles and his pesky followers out of the MegaMall, so Burt could rule. Now because of the Crazies and their stupid flags and banners, the powers are chasing him instead. The forces of Amos Zozz are out to get him. He's sure of it, and he's running scared.

How does he know? The people in black, for one thing. Ever since the trouble, people or things in black have been following him, although whether they're in black uniforms or black Security gear or funeral parlor outfits or pelts of fur, he isn't sure. They're always *there,* always out of sight.

Everywhere Burt goes, they are. If they are people. He doesn't know. All he sees is large shapes, darting shadows— movement that he catches out of the corner of his eye. By the time he whips his head around to check, they've vanished. Did Amos Zozz send them? Zozzco? Or is it something scarier? Burt knows there are other gangs of kids out there somewhere in the MegaMall, and nobody bothers *them.* It isn't fair!

This is all this kid Stiles's fault. Burt and his tribe were *this close* to delivering the girl, after which he was certain the big man would thank him. He and Amos would get to be friends and Burt would be the real insider then. He'd be hanging out with The Power, and Tick could go hang.

Well, Tick wrecked that. The Crazies waved their stupid flags and banners at the cameras like the red flag in front of— what is it, the cow? Whatever! Security came boiling out and there's been trouble ever since. Shadows following, that stop when he stops and move when he moves. Certain things he finds just when he thinks he's safe in the hideout. Strange objects. Crossed sticks. A bloody razor. Face it, they're out to get him.

They want him down in the Dark Hall, he just knows.

Got to do something! The big question is, what?

Burt is angry with Tick, unless he's mad at himself, for getting into this. He is also scared. He doesn't know if he's out to kill the Crazies for messing him up like that, or if he wants to track them down and beg for help.

Ack, it is confusing! Whatever he does, he'd better do it fast, he thinks, running hard. Worried, wild and distracted, Burt Arno is rushing into the wrong place at exactly the wrong time.

Everybody knows you go miles to avoid the Zozzco offices, but Burt is in a hurry. This is exactly where he is right now. He's taking a dangerous short cut through the biz sector of Amos Zozz's commercial empire. This is where the brains of the business are housed. Computers. Accountants. Piles of money, for all he knows. It's a risky half hour after closing time. Oh, yes he is cutting it close. Doesn't he know better? Doesn't he *know* the management people work late? Without Mag here to tell him these things, he doesn't know much. OK, he forgot how dumb it is to be here, where any executive can pop out and catch him. Now that he's banished her, Burt forgets a lot of things.

He doesn't want to admit that Mag is the brains of his operation, but without her, everything's a tad bit harder to keep track of. Like, whether she quit the Dingos or he kicked her out of the tribe. Face it, Mag was his chief of operations, and now look. So this is her fault, for losing the captive. Unless it's Tick's.

That's Strike Two, Tick Stiles. First you missed the Big Faceoff in the Montecassino Courtyard, which makes Burt look bad in front of his people. Then you lost me the girl. You'll pay. Everybody but Burt Arno has forgotten the Big Faceoff, but Burt remembers. It's burning a hole in his belly. His big moment, up in smoke. He and Tick were supposed to parley that night. Tick would turn over the territory and everything the Crazies possessed to make up for the insult, count on it. The peaceable jerk would give it all up— food, money, electronics— that kid would empty his pockets if he had to, anything to keep the peace. They were *this close*. Burt was feeling way good about it, until the girl and Security and the whole bad thing.

Now look. Burt wants war, or something. He needs this meeting! It's like being in the middle of a sneeze that you can't finish. Aaah. He keeps waiting for the *choo*.

Hang tough, he thinks, going along in a muddle. Mag would know what to do. Never should have let her go. Muddle, he thinks muddily, mud, mud, muddle, what'll, what'll I do . . .

This is Burt, trudging through the office corridors.

He looks up. Yikes, the office corridors!

What was I thinking?

Lucky for him the doors are all closed and the corridor is empty. The Zozzco office staff probably packed up and went home for the night. He did a dumb thing, taking this route, but for the moment, he's safe.

Get Tick Stiles, he thinks muddily, *get him good*. Burt Arno thinking is like thawing meat. It takes a while. He still isn't sure exactly, but, hey! *First, get even*. He makes an excited little hop. Idea! *Then get him on my side.*

Cheered, Burt goes a little faster. His trot turns into a kind of jig that keeps him zigzagging from side to side in the narrow corridor. He skips along. Grinning, he raises his right foot in the red canvas Chuckie and taps the wall with his toe.

Zip. Nice. Skip to the other side. Tap with the left foot in the green Chuckie.

Right. Tap. Take that, Crazies.

Left. Tap. Take that, Tick Stiles.

Right. Bonk. And this is for everybody in the Dark Hall. Oh, I don't mean you, Mr. Zozz!

Left. Bonk. He is feeling better.

Right. Actually, he's feeling pretty good! Get help and get even. No, get even and get help. By this time Burt Arno is humming. *The heck with Mag, I can do this.* Improved, he goes along tapping and bonking his sneakers against the walls. *I don't need her at all.* By the time he hits the end of the corridor he's on a roll and, lunging to make that parting left-hand tap, he misses the wall completely and comes tumbling into the marble courtyard where . . .

WHAM. He sprawls.

Oh, noooo!!!

Burt has skidded out of hiding, tripped and fallen into the middle of something very big. This is a Very Important Meeting. Even Burt can tell.

Above the fountain in the executive courtyard at the center of the biz sector, a monster Zozzco banner hangs. There are at least forty people sitting in gilt bamboo chairs around the fountain, and Burt knows from the number of stripes that they are important. Only the bigwigs in Zozzco get a stripe, according to Mag, who keeps track of these things for him. These people all have three or four. They must be very big deals. Still!

In a sea of black Zozzco uniforms, one person stands out.

In the middle of the sea of black stands a tall, elegant figure dressed in dazzling white. The gold stripes on her sleeve go all the way up to the elbow. She stands at a lectern in front of a pyramid of golden Zs topped by a gold dollar sign. She is addressing her minions.

"Zozzpeople!" she cries.

Everyone bows.

What is it about this tall, really important woman in her gold platform shoes that looks so . . . What? Familiar!

Sprawled on the marble where anybody who happens to look down will see him, Burt looks up. Right, her picture was in his reader, back when he used to go to school. And . . . Where else? Wow. In that gi-normous painting in the Castertown Town Hall.

Standing up there, in person, is the legendary Isabella Zozz. The face of Zozzco. The power who stands in front of the power that runs this fabulous shopping world.

The woman is so famous that the very thought makes Burt dizzy. *Me in the same place as Isabella Zozz.*

In Castertown, this is as close as you get to seeing the gods. The only thing scarier would be coming face-to-face with the reclusive founder of the Castertown MegaMall, the legendary Amos Zozz.

Lucky for Burt that the amplifiers are on high. Applause drowned out the noise just now, when he tripped and fell flat on the marble floor.

This means instead of turning to see him squirming to

safety, the Zozzpeople keep staring up at their leader. Visible for miles, Isabella Zozz is tremendous. Like a statue. So perfect that it's scary. Nobody this perfect can be real. She positively gleams in the spotlight. So do the stripes on her sleeve.

"Whatever Zozz wants," she says in a huge voice.

Forty people shout as one, "Whatever Zozz wants."

"And whatever he requires."

They rumble in unison, "Whatever he requires."

"Whatever it takes!"

They seem to be sighing, at least a little bit. "Whatever it takes."

"And what we say here stays here."

"Stays here."

"And." Her voice drops to a deep, thrilling note. "Nobody learns our secrets."

The crowd echoes, "Nobody."

"Pain of death," she says.

"Pain of death." This comes out in a single ominous roar.

Burt doesn't mean to groan. It just comes out. "Agh!"

Nothing happens. Nobody moves. They are too mesmerized to hear!

Shivering, Burt crawls into the shadow of an ornamental planter. Like a trapped panther he crouches, peering out through the fronds of a big dieffenbachia. He is trying not to breathe.

He has caught the Zozzpeople in the middle of the biggest moment of their lives.

"Now, the corporation is in the black," Isabella Zozz says, "and you are all richer than you have ever been.

Now. Do this right and you will be even richer." Her voice drops to a thrilling whisper. "There is always *one notch higher* that you can rise!"

"One notch higher." The suits split the air with the company battle cry. "One notch higher."

"One more stripe to gain!" She touches the emblem on her collar. "And in the end, you may even win the golden Z!"

"The golden Z!"

"For excellence." Isabella raises her fist. "For Zozzco!"

Forty fists rise. "For Zozzco!"

"For survival," she adds, but nobody wants to hear. "Now, we've tried to put this off," Isabella says when the echoes die, "but what Amos wants, Amos gets."

The group repeats, "Amos gets."

"Now," she announces, "about Phase Two."

Awed and frightened, forty people whisper, "Phase Two."

Isabella is so stern that Burt flinches. "This means we must all be very, very careful. Listen to me now, and listen hard." Raking the hall with her eyes, she points a long finger, shouting, "WHATEVER YOU DO, WATCH OUT FOR SPIES!"

Burt flinches.

"STARTING NOW!"

Spies! Burt's belly shrivels.

"If you see one," she growls, "hunt down and destroy."

He can't keep holding his breath. He has to keep holding his breath. If he moves, the plants will start shaking and they will catch him then, for sure.

A mutter runs through the crowd. "Spies, spies, what kind of spies?"

Isabella does not answer. Instead she says, "You'll know them when you see them. Feral. Hidden. Here."

Burt doesn't know what "feral" means, but he knows she is talking about him. The kids. His gang. All the gangs. He has to escape. He has to warn them, but how?

"But that's not the real reason we're here," she says, and Burt gives a little sigh of relief. "Now. My father's agenda."

"Agenda." Worried, they mutter, *budda-budda-budda*. The Zozzco executives sit taller in their seats, waiting to be told.

"Item one." With the next word, Isabella electrifies the room. "If."

Burt is about to die here under the plants. If they don't finish soon, he will die of holding still.

"**If** you want to make it to Phase Two . . ." Isabella Zozz looks down at her notes. When she looks up, she is troubled. "You might as well know, not everyone will make it to Phase Two."

A group gasp of shock rocks the hall.

"First," she says, "you will be judged. On sales. On performance. Production. On your profit line on the merit chart. There will be fitness reports. And if you don't measure up . . ."

"We lose our stripes!" They moan, "Oh, nooooo."

She says darkly, "You will lose more than that."

"Noooooo."

"You will be judged by your fitness reports. And," she says before anybody can ask questions, "on the last day there will be certain tests."

"Tests?" "Fitness reports." Her people fret: *budda-budda-budda,* "Tests . . . tests . . ." They ask, "What kind of tests?"

"Never mind. Just prepare for the day. Now." Isabella leans forward, putting all her weight on her knuckles. "Repeat after me. What Amos wants . . ."

Desperate to please, the suits mutter, "What Amos wants . . ."

"Amos gets."

Then Isabella says the scariest thing yet: "Meanwhile."

They shudder. "Meanwhile."

"He wants us to get rid of superfluous prisoners."

Prisoners! Burt's head comes up so fast that it smacks the dieffenbachia and the plant topples backwards into the flower bed. *Is that what he has in the Dark Hall? Prisoners? What kind of prisoners? Bad kids.* He gulps. *Bad kids like . . .* Gulp. *Like me?* All the bushes in the planter shake like frantic cheerleaders. Burt is so upset that he doesn't see the shadows closing in on him until the great voice of Isabella Zozz splits the air: "Grab him!"

The fake plants part and strong hands close on him.

FIFTEEN

IT'S DEATHLY QUIET IN the MegaMall. The closing bell rang at nine and the last cleaning crews hopped on trams and headed back to their cars an hour ago. The guards in every sector made their rounds and retreated to their steel-plated guard stations behind artificial plants so thick that the public never knows.

Jule is creeping along behind Tick Stiles. They have just slipped into a gallery she's never seen before, not in all the years she's been coming to the MegaMall. Models in sable and mink and sassy fox jackets pose behind safety glass in store windows framed in malachite and jade. On an island that runs along the central corridor, lifelike leopards and raccoons and glistening black bears roam. Only the very rich shop here.

She whispers, "Where are we going?"

Tick says over his shoulder, "Foraging. You don't have to whisper. The surveill cameras just watch, they don't listen."

They are deep inside the Fur Fantasies sector, where ordinary people can't afford to shop. Scouting at closing time, Willie spotted a bonanza in the Polar Bear Food

Court. There's an abandoned microwave in back of Patis-
serialto and outside Delmonico's, a case of steak dinners— a
week's worth of hot meals for the tribe. Now Tick and Jule
have come with a tennis net to snare the goods and drag
them back over marble floors slicker than blown glass.

Suddenly Tick grunts. "Duck. Surveillcam."

In the week she has spent with Tick and his Crazies,
Jule has learned to do as their leader says. For the first time
in perhaps forever, she's part of a group. Feisty and independent as she is, she's learning that she is not her own
master. To get along here, she has to play with the team.

The rangy boy with the dark hair and the wild grin is
in charge here, and to make it in the MegaMall— and she
has to make it in the MegaMall because she's afraid to go
back to that empty house— to make it in the MegaMall,
she has to duck when Tick says so, help gather food and
take care of the smalls, who are too young to take care of
themselves. An only child with an only aunt for company,
she's beginning to like playing with the team. The more
she's here, the more she likes Tick, and the more she likes
Tick, the easier it is to do what he says. She . . .

"Freeze," Tick says, and she freezes.

As the red eye of the surveill camera sweeps across
their path, they turn to stone. Jule still isn't used to the
idea that they are being watched. She imagines a hundred
guards like falcons glaring at a hundred dozen screens,
waiting to pounce. She says through her teeth, "They really don't watch all the time?"

"Not unless they see something move."

"Why aren't they watching?"

"They think they're watching, but they're lazy." The camera moves on and he dodges into the food court with Jule on his heels. At the top step of a sunken area as blue as a polar bears' wading pool, Tick stops to complain. "They're using all these backup things that weren't in the original plans."

"How do you know they weren't in the original plans?"

He doesn't answer; he just goes on. "They put locked gates between sectors. Electrified bars, if you touch one, ZAP. Gas. Jail, for all I know. It wasn't supposed to be this way."

"What wasn't?"

"The Security system."

Jule says, "Wait a minute. You mean they weren't supposed to come at us with nets and bats?"

"They weren't supposed to come at you at all." Tick scowls. "That system was set up to take care of people, not hurt them."

"Who says so?"

Tick grimaces. Remembering. "My dad. There were supposed to be headquarters in every sector, nice walk-in places you could go to if you got hurt or if you happened to get lost and didn't know what to do," he says sadly. He looks into his hands and then looks up. "I think my folks designed Security too."

"You said they were architects."

"They did what Zozzco said."

"So did mine." Bells start going off inside Jule's head. Strangers in the house after she went to bed. The disturbance in the night. *When I woke up they were gone.* She sits down with a thud. "They were happy designing cedar chests until somebody paid them to design something bigger, and . . . How could they?"

Tick sighs. "I guess they didn't want us to be poor. They did whatever he wanted and now they're gone."

"They did what he wanted and one night the big black car came." She is buzzing with pain. "When I woke up they were gone."

Tick sits down next to her on the step, close enough to let her know he cares. "Are you OK?"

"Not really." It takes Jule a minute to gather herself to ask. It comes out in a rush. "What if Zozzco took them?"

"Yours or mine?"

"Both of ours." This is so scary that she shudders. "They all worked for Zozzco and . . . Aunt Christy. She works— worked— for Zozzco until she disappeared, we got MegaMall discounts and free passes, until . . . Until last Monday. Oh. Oh, wow."

"Do you think they took her?"

"Unless she got sick of me and ran away. She's just as gone." Jule sighs. "She was pretty mad about that phone."

"Right. You thought it was your fault," Tick says. "I thought if I was a good boy they'd come back for me."

She looks up. "You thought it was your fault too."

"I did."

"It was never our fault," Jule says.

"No." Tick is quiet for a minute. He is considering. He says carefully, "If Zozzco took our folks, what did they do with them?"

"You mean, did they hurt them or did they take them away or what?"

"It's the *or what* that scares me." Tick leans closer. His voice drops to a whisper even though there's nobody around. "What if they're still here?"

"Here in the mall?"

"Yes. What if . . ."

Jule finishes the thought so fast that it frightens both of them. "What if they're trapped in the Dark Hall?"

Absorbed, Jule and Tick are careless where they should be vigilant. They should have heard soft footsteps approaching. They should have seen the wiry, barefooted stranger dart out from behind the concession stands above the arctic dining area and slide down the artificial snowbank that rings the artificial pond, but they didn't. They're too deep in their own thoughts to notice as the shadow moves behind the plastic evergreens that ring the curved steps where they are sitting. On the glazed blue surface of the pretend pond in front of them, everything is still. Frosted stools and tables sit in the marble dining area like floating blocks of ice.

Grimly, Tick repeats, "The Dark Hall."

"Guys." It's so loud and sudden that they both jump. "Guys!"

Jule whirls. "Who?"

"Guys." The girl's red hair is wild and her eyes are full of what she has to tell them. "Listen, guys!"

Jule's on her feet before Tick. At the sight of the short, furious little redhead, all that bad business with the Dingos comes rushing back. "Mag!"

Tick turns. "You know this girl?"

"You bet I do. That's Mag Sullivan, she works for Burt."

"Not any more."

Jule remembers Mag gripping the Kryptonite lock, shoving her along. She remembers Mag's fingers locked in her hair. "Who says so?"

"Are you going to shut up and listen, or what?"

"Don't trust her," Jule says. "Watch out."

Mag snaps, "No, you watch out. This is important."

"Watch out for her, I mean it. You can't trust her, she's a Dingo girl."

She bares her teeth at Jule. "I told you, not any more."

"Don't lie to us." Jule gives Mag a push.

Mag pushes back. "Get over yourself."

"You're not taking me back to the Dingos." Jule punches Mag's arm. "And that's that!"

Then Mag Sullivan grabs Jule by the shoulders and turns her around so they are facing. "Don't be stupid. When the guards came down, who do you think let you go?"

Tick says quietly, "I saw you and your gang with Jule, you had her tied up. So, where were you taking her?"

"Dark Hall," Mag says. "That is, Burt was. I don't know what he thought he was doing, he was all about a sacrifice. Like that would change everything for us."

"Sacrifice!"

"Then you came along."

"I did not, he caught me!"

"Burt said catching you was, like, a humongous gift. The next thing I knew we were on the march."

"I was a sacrifice?" Jule is upset. "Sacrifice to what?"

It hurts Mag to say, "If I knew, I'd tell you. Do you believe I was trying to help you escape?"

"How do I know what you were trying to do?"

"Do I look too weak to hang on to you?" Even Jule can see that Mag is all muscle.

The little redhead turns to Tick. "Do you believe Burt wants to get rid of you guys?"

He nods. "That, I believe."

"Revenge, or something worse. That's why I quit."

Jule says, "I bet he kicked you out."

"And now you're asking to join up with us." Tick is counting on his fingers. Mouths to feed, maybe. Places to sleep. "I don't know if . . ."

"Don't be a jerk. I don't want to join you, I came to warn you."

Mag and Tick begin a fast exchange— new girl and tribe leader, who asks: "Warn us. About Burt?"

"No. About a lot of things. I've been on my own for a week now, and I've been exploring. There's more going on in this place than you know about."

Tick nods. "We know."

"You only think you know," Mag says ominously. "Do you know they've been meeting in a different sector every night?"

"They?"

"The suits. The old man's Zozzpeople. Like, the brains behind this operation. Something big is coming up."

Still stewing over that march to the Dark Hall, Jule elbows her. "I suppose you know exactly what this big thing is and when it's going to happen."

Mag spits, "I wish! They've got some kind of orders to do something with . . ."

Jule spits words back at her. "Yeah, orders. Yeah, right."

"Don't fight." Tick puts himself between them. "We have to work together here."

"OK then," Jule says. *Play with the team.* She sighs. "Right."

Mag finishes, ". . . the prisoners."

This makes Jule gasp. "Prisoners! Prisoners?"

Mag doesn't stop to explain; she rushes on to the important news. "Do you know there's an underground river?"

Tick says, "A river?"

But Jule is hung up on what Mag just said. She presses, "What prisoners?"

"Yeah," Mag tells Tick, "you know the river in Castertown? It starts underneath this place."

Jule murmurs, "Prisoners," but the other two have moved on.

"A river!" Tick's eyes catch fire. "Where does it go?"

"That's the whole thing! I found it my first night out on my own. When you're alone," Mag says, scowling, "when you don't have a hideout you can't sleep days, like normal kids. You have to spend all day running around the mall. So you sleep nights instead. I sleep underneath a bench in the Hall of Beauty, you know, the one with all the hair weaving and makeup and mini face-lift shops? Burt would never look for me there. My first night on the floor I heard water. I thought I heard water rushing under there."

"It's a river, or you only think it's a river?"

Glowering, Mag shoves a wet sleeve into Tick's face. "I know it is.

"That night I just listened. Then I started tracing it, you know, to the loudest point? Tonight I found it and I went down." Mag's eyes are so wide that even Jule knows she's telling the truth. "That river starts underneath this place, and it's *humongous*. I think it's the secret to everything. It's how certain things get to town and how certain people get out of here — you know, when you stop seeing them, and it might be why when bad stuff happens, nobody in Castertown complains."

"What do you mean?"

She rushes on, "But that isn't the important thing."

Jule's mind is still running after the prisoners, but she knows better than to interrupt. She is listening intently now.

Mag finishes. "Look. I know how to get down."

"Ten years." Tick is shaking his head. "Ten years and I never knew."

"The Hall of Beauty, get it? It's not like guys would go there in a million years. I heard water running and went down a ladder to explore." Mag shakes herself like a dog. "I fell in."

"How . . ."

"I moved the right trash barrel and lifted the right grate."

"A grate!" Jule looks at Tick. Why is he surprised?

"You know about the grates under the trash barrels, right?"

Tick shakes his head.

Jule says, "I do."

Mag grins at her. "Now tell me you ran into Lance."

"Ski mask, camo jacket? He rescued me!"

"Me too." Mag says mysteriously, "He lives down there."

"In the service corridors," Tick says.

"No. On the river."

Tick rubs his head, bemused. "All these years and he never told me."

Mag turns. "You didn't know?"

"No." After some thought Tick says, "You can live here ten years and not know a lot of things."

"Tell me about it." Mag grins. "I didn't know there was a river, and I've only been here for a month."

Jule is beginning to like Mag in spite of herself. "How did you get here?"

"Ran away from the State Home with Burt and them."

"State Home!"

"We ended up here."

"What were you doing in the State Home?"

Mag gives Jule a dark look. "That's where they put you when you don't have anybody to take care of you."

"That's what I'm afraid of."

Mag is saying, "But you wouldn't know."

Jule shudders. "Oh yes I would."

"Would not."

Tick's hand chops the air between them. "Stop that! OK, Mag. Tell us what you found."

"Right." Mag is talking directly to Tick. "OK, so. It was dark down there; none of those tramway lights. No tram tracks!"

"That's crazy."

"Turned out the ladder ran straight down to the river, but I didn't know until too late. I fell in. It was awful. I floated for, like, hours." The memory pulls Mag's face apart. "If it hadn't been for Lance . . . Lance pulled me out of the water and took me back to his cave."

"Cave!"

"Sort of. Hideout, I think. He built it out of leftover stuff. He fed me and while I was eating, he told me a couple of things." She turns to Tick. "He told me to tell you."

"Like what?"

Mag isn't ready to answer. "Then he rowed me back to the ladder where I fell in. Now, Lance and I are friends, at least as good as it gets with Lance, but at the top of the ladder he opened this trap and . . ." Her face tightens in an angry glare. "He kicked me out. Then he slammed it on me and bolted it shut. And here I thought we were friends."

Tick prods her. "And he wanted me to know . . ."

At last she tells him in a rush of words. "The river comes out of the ground underneath the Dark Hall."

Tick looks at Jule and Jule looks at Tick but neither says what's running through their heads in neon block letters: *WHERE I THINK MY PARENTS ARE*. They could be. They could! Tick prompts, "And it goes . . ."

"Straight to Castertown. And there's another thing."

They wait for what seems like forever for Mag to finish.

When she has their full attention, Mag says, "They've been putting something in the water."

Jule whispers, "You mean in *our river*?"

"Barrels of stuff that they pour in. It's doing something to the people."

"What?"

"I don't know, he just said tell you he can't do it alone

and it has to stop. He said tell you they're getting rid of the prisoners, and . . ."

"OK." Tick flips open his phone. He is texting Willie, James. "OK!"

"We have to hurry." Mag's face squinches up. "He says something awful is coming down. Hurry," Mag says, moving off before they can ask questions or get answers.

"Wait!"

But Mag is running. "Come on." All this and finally she gets to the point. "They got Burt."

SIXTEEN

AMOS IS IN THE inmost, secret command module, tapping the master screen as though he can pick up the shoppers captured by the cameras yesterday and move them around in the box. He's so excited he is singing, "Spring and summer, winter, fall. Cool kids shop at the MegaMall."

Soon this jingle will be playing in all the major cities of the world. Amos is poised to move on, into Phase Two.

"Spring and summer, winter, fall. Cool kids shop at the MegaMall." The warped tycoon knows better than anyone that when you control people's wallets, you control them. Money speaks louder than all the bombs and artillery in the world.

"Spring and summer . . ."

With the commercials, he lured them, and now . . . Plastered to his walls are years' worth of MISSING posters, piled layer upon layer— pictures and details on adults, children, all reported missing in the countless sectors of the MegaMall. These are the old man's trophies. Gleefully, he sings, "Spring and summer . . ."

At his back, Isabella clears her throat.

Amos jumps. Caught in the act! Quickly, he claps on the gray mask that he wears to meet family. "You took long enough."

Full of self-importance, she says, "Something came up. It's seriously grave," and then stands there, waiting for Amos to ask.

When you get right down to it, he doesn't much like Isabella. He never did. She is a necessary evil, at least until this part of the operation is done. He put her in power because the last thing Amos Zozz wants to do is meet the public looking the way he does. What if somebody ripped off his mask? Dozens of years and millions of dollars' worth of plastic surgery and he looks worse than ever. His lumps are bigger. His bumpy head is just as bald. He can still hear the children's ugly laughter. The wasps and the glue he had to use after the Galt twins ripped off his wig all those years ago destroyed his scalp. He can't stand anything on his head.

He will get even with them, he is in the process. He has people working around the clock. He has the ultimate checklist in place. The big day is approaching and all his fool daughter can talk about is this wretched meeting she just had.

Right now, Isabella is boasting. "I'm a very motivational speaker, Dad. I had them eating out of my hand! And then. And then!" Preening, she buffs her fingernails on her gold stripes. "You'll never guess what happened, Dad."

"Don't call me Dad."

Her proud face hardens. "But, Dad!"

"Stop that. You came out of a test tube." He only had Isabella to carry on the family name, and look how that turned out. His daughter is so vain that he had to pay her to get married and double the amount to lose her figure long enough to give him an heir.

"Father, it's important."

"Don't." The boy was his living image, a proper figure-head for the corporation. Beautiful hair, Amos had such hopes. Well, look how that turned out. With his designated heir a disgrace to the family, he's stuck with Isabella here. "No more babies," she told him, although he promised bil-lions if she'd give him a backup grandson. With a sniff she said, "I have my figure to think about." How can he expect this woman to run a corporation when her looks are all she cares about? But Isabella doesn't know what he is thinking.

"Really important."

"Think of yourself as the family logo," he says sourly. "The face of Zozzco . . ."

"Sure, Father," Isabella says. "But wait'll I tell you . . ."

Amos adds, just loud enough for Isabella to hear, ". . . for now." That silences her. He needs this daughter, but he doesn't like her. When this is done, he'll have to dispose of her. To think that he had the most beautiful mask in his office made in the image of that grandson, the ungrateful little toad. *He looked like me,* he thinks. *No.* His throat fills with the same old bitterness, as if a million hornets are boiling in his brain. *The way I would have looked.* Now that the boy is out of the picture, there's not a lot of family feeling left in Amos Zozz. "Isabella, the checklist."

"But this is important."

"Later. The checklist." Stupid girl. She married a handsome man as ordered and, as ordered, she let Amos kick him out when he'd done his part. Then she dropped the ball. She didn't care about the baby, she cared about getting her figure back. The woman was so focused on the mirror, *so focused on her looks,* Amos thinks resentfully, that she fell down on the job. She should have taught that child to love the corporation, to follow Amos without question; she should have taught him that power is everything, and that power comes from control.

"But Da— Father— Mr. Zozz!"

If only the boy . . . Don't ask him about the boy. "Isabella, focus! We're going over the checklist now."

"Please!"

He hates that he has to stand on his toes to glare into her face. If Amos is a little bit jealous of Isabella's looks, he won't admit it. Not even to himself. Isabella is efficient but foolish, he thinks bitterly. All vanity— that lovely hair . . . Never mind. He needs her, at least until the Phase Two launch. He taps the clipboard, ready to take her down the To-Do list. "Item one!"

"All right," Isabella says grudgingly. Her tone says, *All right for yooouuuu.*

Amos ticks off the first item. "Prisoners."

Isabella says vaguely, "Working on it."

"Construction."

"Working on it."

They go down the items one by one. Isabella's answers are unsatisfactory, every one. Everything has to be done according to the plan Amos started laying as a boy, the plan he has honed and perfected and brooded over day and night ever since. The MegaMall is his triumph, but it's only Phase One. Certain key people know about Phase Two, but the final, delicious touch, Amos keeps secret. He has stored up the details all his life until now, hoarding them like gold.

His Zozzpeople don't know it, but they've been working toward the old man's biggest moment for years. Still, his idiot daughter is half-listening, half-answering. She seems to be more interested in whatever fool thing she was trying to tell him. This won't do!

To bring her into line Amos barks, "Now. About the employee fitness reports."

Just when he thinks he's cowed her, Isabella falls silent.

"I said, *What about the fitness reports?*"

Instead of answering like a good girl, she rocks on the wedges of her tall gold shoes, swelling with importance. "Father, there's something you really have to know."

True ruler of the MegaMall, king of the jungle in any world, the outraged Amos snarls, "There's nothing I don't know."

"You don't know this." Isabella bends down so she is breathing directly in his face. As Amos draws back, she whispers as if telling an awful secret, "There are feral children in the MegaMall."

She knows. But she doesn't know everything. Amos produces a showy yawn. "Don't waste my time."

"Father!" Isabella is huffing with excitement. "We caught one."

His head comes up. *Never mind,* he thinks. *She'll find*

out the truth anyway, when I reveal the master plan. He tries not to let her know that he's excited. "And?"

"What shall I do with him?"

"Bring him to me. And don't call me Father!" In his thoughts, Amos is running on ahead. The minute Isabella leaves here, he'll organize the roundup, but the mean, secret part of him doesn't want Isabella to know what he's up to until the last minute. Knowledge is power. Clearing his throat, he says, "Now, about your to-do list. Isabella, **These things must be done.**"

"But Father . . ."

"Don't call me Father!" Amos takes his voice to a place it's never been before, at least not in front of anybody, rasping, "Now, finish by Friday or I'll finish you."

"I'M WORKING ON IT!" she shouts angrily, and stamps out on those ridiculous golden shoes.

Alone, Amos runs from monitor to monitor, touching the surfaces as though he could pluck out the shoppers running like ants and crush them in his hands. *Control.* The hunger is rising. He is overwhelmed by the need. It takes shape in his mouth and bubbles out in the same words the furious, wounded boy sputtered all those years ago, with his scalp raw and his warped body covered with bumps from a thousand stingers, poisoned by hatred more toxic than the venom of a million hornets.

Helpless with rage, the richest man in the world makes his threat in the most powerful words he can find for what he is feeling.

How would he feel if he knew they were the same words used by foolish, bullheaded Burt Arno?

Because he was trapped and hurt by children, those

snide, smelly, heartless little monsters, because he can't show his face and the top of his naked head still hurts, *because they made him look this way,* he hates them all.

He hates children beyond all hating; he despises them beyond reason. He *will* get even, and now the time is near.

Frothing with rage, Amos roars, "I WILL MAKE THEM PAY."

SEVENTEEN

PUPPY."

Doakie is lost. He only came down in the tunnels because Puppy ran away. He promised not to leave the new hideout without a big kid along. Nance and Jiggy will be so mad!

Well FOO on them. This is all their fault. He heard Puppy crying so he followed the *hrr hrrr* and now he is down here.

"Puppy?"

Tick says be a good boy and whatever you do stay out of the tunnels, but Doakie isn't scared. With the little orange lights on the railroad tracks it isn't *so* dark in here.

The only scary part is, he is alone. Plus his baby Scottie is just as black as the cement so he might be hard find.

Never mind, he always comes when Doakie calls. He goes along the ledge in the tunnel, calling, "Puppy?"

He doesn't hear Puppy any more.

He says into the hush, "Puppy?"

Jiggy and Nance are gonna kill him. Everybody else got to go out tonight, but Nance and Jiggy aren't allowed.

Doakie had the sniffles so Tick told them to keep care of him.

"Puppy?"

Jiggy and Nance have to stay back because they got Tick in trouble with the Dingos. So, that was way last week, but Tick is still mad at them! Tick says Jiggy and Nance are under House Arrest until he says so.

They started saying mean things about Tick as soon as he and that cranky new girl went out the door.

Doakie wasn't doing anything, but Nance and Jiggy were mean to him. They said it was his fault they were stuck in here babysitting when they wanted to play. Then they started pinging paper clips at him. Ow. Ow! When he wouldn't cry they pinged paper clips at Puppy instead. They couldn't hit Puppy so they used bikkies to call him and, yow, they got the leash on him. Then Nance held him and Jiggy pulled back the rubber band with a great big paper clip aimed at Puppy's head.

Doakie yelled, "Don't hurt him," but they didn't care.

Then Puppy nipped this mean girl Nancy and she hollered and let go. He started yip-yipping and running in circles and Nance and Jiggy laughed and laughed. Then Puppy scooted through their legs and into the back room where the tunnel steps are. Doakie tried to fall on the leash to stop him but Puppy got away.

Tick told the smalls never to go into the service tunnels without a big kid along, but he has to find Puppy! Doakie tried to pretend Puppy was hiding in the back room, but he wasn't. He could hear him *hrr-hrrring* at the bottom of the stairs and he took a deep breath and jumped. Now Doakie is in the tunnel. Poor Puppy, running around down here in the dark, dragging his leash. If anything bad gets Puppy, Doakie will die.

Now Jiggy and Nance have quit yelling and started hunting him but Doakie doesn't care. Tick will kill them if they leave the hideout, so they can't get down here. They wouldn't dare. Tick will probably kill him too, for running away, but he had to save Puppy, right?

If only he could *find* him!

"Puppy?"

When Tick comes back and finds out Doakie's gone, he will give Nance and Jiggy holy heck. Serves them right for hurting his brand-new baby dog.

"Puppy? Come on, Puppy." When nobody answers, Doakie squinches his face up and calls the name Tick said was on his collar. "MacTavish?"

Tick says Puppy is a Scotch terrier so we can't just call him Puppy. He has a Scottish name. Tick calls him Mac-Tavish, but he never comes. He only comes to Doakie so Doakie knows Puppy is his dog, and no matter what Tick says, Puppy is his real and only name.

"Puppy?"

He hears Puppy crying. It's coming from somewhere far away. Doakie holds his nose like he does when Daddy puts him in the swimming pool? Or like he used to before Doakie got lost and Tick found him and he started living here. Then he hops down off the ledge and lands on his knees. He gets up and starts running along beside the track calling his dog. He's about to give up when he hears that *hrr hrrr* again and oh my gosh here's Puppy, jumping up and down and wagging to beat the band.

"Puppy! Why didn't you come?"

Puppy jerks at his leash and starts going, *Hrr hrrr.* His leash got caught on one of the spokes in the track.

"Oh Puppy, Puppy!" Doakie kneels in the gravel and hugs Puppy and Puppy wriggles and squeaks, he is so happy to see Doakie again, and then he jumps up and licks Doakie's face.

The leash is pretty much stuck under the railroad track, Puppy's been pulling so hard trying to get away, and Doakie and the baby Scottie are both so excited that Doakie keeps tugging instead of doing like a smart boy would, which is take off Puppy's collar and pick him up and run home before anybody comes along. There is the sound of a tram coming down the track from a long way off and by the time Doakie finally undoes the collar and grabs Puppy in his arms, it sounds really really close.

It is close, too close, and Doakie shrinks back into the cement wall of the tunnel hoping nobody's looking and whoever's riding on the tram will just go on by without noticing, but he can't hold his breath forever and the tram isn't just zooming by, it's going really slowly and it's practically on top of him.

Doakie scrunches down and tries not to be here. He wants to see who's riding on it but he thinks maybe if he closes his eyes real tight they won't see him.

There are voices rising over the sound of the iron wheels, grownups talking.

Don't move, Doakie. Don't look.

Scrunched down with his eyes shut tight, Doakie starts holding his breath. Maybe they'll just roll on by. He's holding it so hard that his fingers twitch and Puppy starts wiggling.

Then Doakie's eyelids go all pink inside. The tram is so close that he can see the headlight right through the skin. If only they don't see him!

Puppy won't stop wiggling! What if he barks? He has to get Puppy by the nose and hold his mouth shut so he doesn't bark or start crying or yip-yipping.

Hrrm hrrm, Puppy says through Doakie's fingers. He is squirming even harder because Doakie is holding so tight that it hurts.

"Shh," Doakie begs. "Be quiet."

Puppy doesn't like Doakie holding his nose. Puppy starts wiggling, he's as slippery as a fish.

"Oh please, Puppy. Please shh."

The tram is really close now. It's moving really slowly, too. It's still rolling, but not fast enough to go away before Puppy starts making noise.

One more minute, Puppy, please!

Then Puppy makes one last wild twist of his little body and escapes! The baby Scottie goes running right straight out onto the track, right into the circle of the tram headlight, bouncing and arf-arf-arfing because he's so happy to be free.

"Oh," Doakie yells, running after him. "Ooooh nooooo!"

The bright light shines right straight in Doakie's eyes, filling them up so he can't see. The car grinds to a stop.

"Puppy," he calls, rubbing his eyes. "Puppy!" Did the train hit him? He doesn't know. Doakie looks around for Puppy but Puppy isn't anywhere. He keeps calling in spite of the men in suits hopping down off the tram and heading his way. "Puppy, are you OK?"

"Grab him," one of the grownups says.

Before Doakie knows what's happened to him he's tied to the back rail of the tram. It is carrying a whole bunch of important people someplace important and oh my gosh, they have great big scary Burt Arno tied down on a seat way up there in the front row. He's tied up between two big important people with lots of stripes. They are arguing like Burt isn't even there. They have Doakie too, but they're so busy talking business that it's like he doesn't exist.

Poor Puppy's back there somewhere, Doakie knows it. Is he OK or did he get mooshed? Puppy ran out on the tracks right in front of the tram and Doakie doesn't know. He doesn't know! Poor Puppy! Puppy is back there in the tunnel and the tram is rolling faster, faster, going away. Even though they tied him down with their belts, he squirms like Puppy until he's turned himself around so he can see out the back.

The grownups tied Doakie up tight so they wouldn't have to think about him, but he is leaning out the back, trying to see as far behind him as he can. He wants to see all the way back down the track to where Puppy was, but it's too far. Doakie doesn't care, he has to keep trying, which is why he and he alone sees something else in the tunnel: Lance the Loner in his leafy spotted pants and his big black mask. Lance on a handcar with great big rubber wheels, silently following behind.

EIGHTEEN

DOAKIE IS NOWHERE NEAR as scared as Burt Arno.

They picked up that guy Tick's favorite little kid about two minutes ago, whereas Burt's been racketing through these dark tunnels for hours. He has no idea where they are right now, the MegaMall's so big and the tunnels are so gnarly, but he does know where they're going.

They are heading for the Dark Hall.

The suits have Burt handcuffed in the front row of a carload of Zozzco executives, all in black except for the gold stripes on the sleeves. After they trapped him at the big meeting the execs swarmed down a hole in the floor and shoveled him into the company tram. Somebody slapped a band of duct tape over his mouth and they started out. They've been riding ever since.

He is flattened between two Zozzco vice presidents who keep leaning over Burt to confer, talking like he's a lump of dough or a bag of dirty laundry or something, not the proud leader of the Dingo tribe, which is what he is.

On a good day, Burt would rage at them: *You can't do this to me!*

Right now he's just scared. Plus, they're talking about him.

In the tram behind him, ten black suits with white, white faces are muttering, *buddabuddabudda*, nonstop. Burt can only pick up a few words at a time. *Buddabudda* ". . . do," he hears, *buddabuddabudda*, ". . . what are we supposed to do?"

"Wait for orders," someone says.

They all talk at once. The *buddabuddabudda* is scary. ". . . something with the prisoners . . ." *buddabuddabudda,* "This prisoner . . ." ". . . do what with the prisoners?"

"Get rid of them!" The Zozzpeople haven't stopped muttering since they grabbed Burt and grappled him into the tram. This isn't as scary as the fact that they all sound scared. *Buddabuddabudda* turns into, ". . . fitness reports."

"Do it or we lose our stripes!"

"What about these kids?"

Kids! Writhing, Burt closes his teeth on a fold of duct tape and grinds down so hard that it shreds. *I am the proud leader of the Dingos, I am not a kid!*

The vice president on his right says, "No big problem, there are only two."

"But . . ."

The vice president on his left commands her partner, "Wait for orders!" It's scary, seeing the woman bare her teeth that way. At that exact minute, her phone rings. She flips it open and everything changes. "It's Amos."

"Amos!" Everybody moans, "Oooooh noooooo . . ."

"It's an All Points Bulletin from Amos. I'm putting him on speakerphone."

The rich and powerful owner's big, deep voice fills the tunnel. "Zozzpeople!"

Around Burt, strong adults crumble.

The old man's voice blasts a hole in the night. "There are feral children loose in my beautiful MegaMall."

"Oooooh noooooo . . ."

"Running through the place in packs," he spits. "Like rats."

Rats! Furious, Burt is working his tongue through the tiny hole he's torn in the duct tape; if he could talk, what would he be yelling? He's so angry that you don't want to know.

"Sir." She glances at Burt, then back at Doakie. "What do you want us to do with them?"

"Round them up," Amos thunders, and everybody jumps. This is particularly scary as they have Burt and Doakie right there in the tram. Amos says coldly, "I have something in mind."

Then the big woman with all the stripes surprises Burt. Instead of saluting or whatever these people do she says, "Sir, they're just children!"

This makes Burt fume. *I'm not* **children**.

"DO AS I SAY!" Amos shrieks, shaking Burt all the way down to the knuckles in his toes. Then the boss hits a level tone that is even more threatening. "If you fail," he says, "you all get F on your fitness reports. AND YOU KNOW WHAT THAT MEANS."

The Zozzpeople don't, exactly, but the threat sends them all into a fit of anxious *buddabuddabudda*-ing, "Catch them," "Have to catch them," "What if we can't catch them." "What if."

Amos's voice rises high enough to overflow the tunnel and sweep away everything and everybody in it. **"UNDERSTOOD?"**

Twelve people snap to attention, shouting, "Understood!"

The VP on Burt's left taps her phone. "He's gone."

The VP on Burt's right looks puzzled. "Catch them and . . ." For a long moment, all the *buddabuddabudda* stops. There is nothing but the *whish* of the tram zipping along the rails.

Out of the hush that follows comes, "And what?"

This is the big question. "What's he going to do with them?"

The people on the tram don't know what he'll do, exactly, but they all know what it means. Burt shrivels up and dies as they chorus, "Anything he wants."

For a long time it is silent in the tram. They are all riding along worrying. Finally someone says what they are all thinking. "What if we can't catch them and bring them in?"

The vice president on the left side of Burt turns and says sharply, "We have to catch them or . . ."

"Have to catch them . . ."

"Catch them . . ."

"Or . . ."

All this *buddabuddabudda* is grating on Burt. He has ripped the tape and as the anxious *buddabuddabudda* rises, he explodes. "Or what," he rages before they can silence him. "Or what?"

Shocked, someone in the back comes out with the truth. "He got tired of the prisoners so he's getting rid of the prisoners. If we can't catch the kids, he'll . . ."

Someone says shakily, "Take away our stripes!"

The woman VP snaps, "You'd better hope that's all he does. If he can't get rid of them, he'll . . ."

There is a gasp and then there is another silence. Like Burt, everybody in the tram is thinking, *Get rid of me?*

Everybody moans at once. "Ohhh, nooooooo!"

All around Burt, Zozzpeople are panicking. Then the VP on the right side of Burt turns and says in a strong voice, "Cheer up, we've already caught two."

The woman VP says firmly, "And the big one's going to lead us to the rest."

Burt spits out the last bit of tape. He bucks and struggles, shouting, "I will not!"

"Oooooh, yes you will!" the VP on Burt's right shouts, so everyone will hear. "Or else."

"Or else what?" Burt is grappling with the other VP—his last words before she slaps fresh tape over his mouth.

Then she says darkly, "You don't want to know."

Somebody says, "We don't know."

"Nobody knows."

In the back, someone asks the real question. "What does he want with these children anyway?"

"Adoption," one says, and somebody else tries, "torture" and grinding away at the tape over his mouth which is now partly inside his mouth, Burt hears, "Clearance sale!"

The *buddabuddabudda* chases itself in circles as they race along, ending at, "sacrifice. Maybe he wants a sacrifice."

They take it up and Burt shudders. "Sacrifice."

Now they are all muttering at once, "Sacrifice!"

Oh, yes this makes Burt anxious and guilty. He had no

idea why he thought he had to make an offering to Amos but that's why he marched the girl toward the Dark Hall: *sacrifice*. He doesn't know what he thought it would get him, only that it seemed like a good idea. He does know that he was thinking *sacrifice* at the time. He is guilty and sorry and scared.

A whisper swells in the air. "What if we fail?"

Everybody gasps. Then everybody groans.

The officials in black uniforms with gold stripes and gold emblems shout as one, "WE MUST NOT FAIL!"

Then, because there's always the possibility that their leader is listening, the VP on Burt's right raises a loyal shout. "Anything for Zozzco."

The one on his left chimes in with a rousing, "Anything for the corporation!"

They all cry, "Everything for the corporation."

"We love the corporation."

The *buddabuddabudda* turns into a little chorus, like song.

Someone whispers, "We love Zozzco . . ."

The vice presidents prompt, "And who else do we love?"

They shout in unison, "AND WE LOVE AMOS ZOZZ!" Loud as they are, the Zozzpeople are uneasy.

"What if he doesn't love us?"

A hush falls. Then they wail, "Don't even *think* it, we have to try!"

The muttering turns desperate. "You can try, but . . ."

". . . but you never know . . ."

Buddabuddabudda, ". . . you never know with Amos Zozz."

Burt shudders.

This is awful.

Unlike Doakie, he knows where they're going.

Worse. He thinks he knows what they're going to do.

You bet he is scared.

NINETEEN

MAG CAN'T UNDERSTAND WHY Tick and his main men are racing through the tunnels, chasing after a stupid dog when they ought to be down on the underground river right now, heading for the Dark Hall.

She can't understand why they aren't rushing to save Burt, although she ought to know. When she told them Burt had been captured, Jule said, "He wanted to hurt me. Why should I care what happens to him?"

Tick added, "You want me to risk everything to save a guy who wants to ruin us?"

"Right," Jule said. "Why should we care when I could care less?"

This, of course, was when Tick surprised her, although Mag already knew how this would come down. As Mag watched, Tick Stiles took this girl Jule by the shoulders and held her in place firmly, to make her listen. "Because that's what kids do for kids. We have to help each other, no matter what."

She started, "Even after he tried to . . ."

"Yes." Tick let her go and stood back. "It's what I do."

OK then, why aren't they already on the river, rushing to rescue Burt? Something awful could happen to him, while they're messing around in the tunnels. He could die!

It's the puppy's fault. Tick and Willie, James and that girl Jule are following this little black furball when they should be on the river this minute, rowing for Burt's life.

"Come on, guys. Could we do this later? Please?"

But the Crazies are chasing that dog. Right when they were fixing to go down the hatch to the bank of the underground river, they heard it. *Arf.* Mag had them all set to go down the ladder in the wishing well in the Hall of Beauty— gear and all— when this baby Scottie bounded in out of nowhere and distracted them. All the Crazies dropped their rafts, pumps and paddles right there in the middle of the Hall of Beauty. Some rescue team!

Stupid puppy. They had the lid halfway off the wishing well and here it came out of nowhere, wagging and barking like a rescue dog with people to save. *Arf.* It jumped up and down, spronkaspronka. *Arf!*

Jule yelled, "Guys. That's Doakie's dog!" *Arf.*

The Crazies forgot all about Burt. "Doakie!"

"Is he all right?"

"Doggie, where's Doakie?" *Arf arf.* The Crazies were running in circles.

"Did Doakie send you? Does he need us?"

"What's the matter, Puppy?"

Arf!

"He's trying to tell us something! It's about Doakie, right?"

Arf. "Is Doakie lost or trapped or something? Is he OK?"

"Wait a minute," Mag yelled. "What about Burt?"

Willie lunged. "Grab him. I think he knows where Doakie is."

James grabbed and the puppy skittered away. "Hurry. He could be hurt."

"He's *fine!*" Mag banged the fake wishing well with an oar to get their attention. "Guys, the river's this way. Doakie will be fine. Hurry. We have to save Burt!"

Instead, Tick went after the stupid dog. "Tavish!"

Then that girl Jule called, "Puppy?" It came to her right away, but every time she reached for it the thing backed out of reach. When she quit following, Puppy turned. *Aren't you coming?* He cocked his head, waiting. Jule said, "He's leading us somewhere!" and they all took out after him.

Now instead of going down the ladder and launching the rafts, like they were supposed to; instead of rescuing Burt, Tick Stiles and his main Crazies are after this stupid dog. Tick, Willie and James and Jule are deep in the service tunnels. If Mag doesn't follow, she'll never get them back on Burt's case. Everybody that ought to be saving Burt is chasing Puppy along the glistening tram track. Like Scotties can talk, and as soon as they catch him the dog will say what's up with this kid Doakie. Yeah, sure.

Burt's in big trouble, she's sure of it. Time is running out, and they are stuck down here. "Guys," Mag calls, but nobody listens. "Guys!"

"Doakie." Their voices fill the dark service tunnel: Tick, James, Willie and Jule, calling, "Are you down here, Doak?"

"Come on, guys," Mag says, "He's probably sitting at home right now—"

They rush on as if she hasn't even spoken. "Doakie? If you can hear me, yell!"

"—laughing at you. He'll wait," Mag says, running along at Tick's elbow. "The Zozzpeople have Burt and that can't wait." Her breath hits a bump and she gulps. "If we don't hurry . . ."

"Later." Turning, Tick shouts, "Doakie, if you can't talk, bang on the rail!"

Mag trails off. ". . . they could torture him."

Tick's voice hits like a rap on the knuckles. "I *said*, later."

"Fine!"

Jule falls back, crouching to peek under loading platforms, while Willie and James shine their lights into side tunnels, calling, "Doak!"

"Girl," Mag says. "Talk to them. They won't listen to me."

Jule says curtly, "Burt can take care of himself."

"You don't know Zozzpeople."

Now Jule's voice hits a strange, dark note that surprises Mag. "That's what you think. Doakie comes first, so help us do this. Then we help Burt."

Mag blames this girl for escaping, which messed her up with the Dingos, but never mind. They are in the same boat now. The two girls run along together, calling, "Doakie? Doak?"

For a long time there are only the tunnels, long and silent and dark. Then they hear loud bark-barking. It's Puppy. He's stopped in the middle of the tracks. He's perched on the rail, barking at them over a blob that could be anything from a ruptured party balloon to a captured rat.

"What's that?"

Grinning, the puppy wags as if he's found something terribly important and is waiting to be praised. Tick turns his light on Puppy's prize. It's Doakie's purple canvas shoe.

Mag says, "Now will you listen? They've got Doakie too."

"Right." Tick whirls so fast that his face blurs.

Jule groans. "The Dark Hall."

Shaken, Tick says, "Or worse. OK, Mag. You're in charge."

"The river starts there," Mag says. "We'd better hurry."

Jule scoops up the puppy. "OK, Mag. Show us the way."

Pushing rafts, paddles, everything that floats, down the well at the Hall of Beauty fountain, the Castertown Crazies set out on the hidden river. Bravely, they push off, with no idea what lies ahead.

TWENTY

THESE ARE HARD TIMES for Lance the Loner. There are places in the mall that Lance is sworn, signed and sealed never to go and there are places he isn't supposed to know about, but he is here.

As always, he is alone. He's been this way ever since he got old enough to make it on his own. Going it alone is his choice, but he's never felt so alone.

To get his freedom from the family, the Zozzco Corporation and everything that it stands for, Lance signed an agreement, and until tonight, he has honored it. He has honored it for all these years. Lance honors the agreement and the people in charge of operations in the MegaMall let him come and go as he likes. All he has to do is flash the key card, but now . . .

He is in one of those places he promised never to be.

He is sitting here thinking.

Push has come to shove, and Lance has to make a choice.

Everything comes down to what he does next.

Where the family is concerned, Lance doesn't exist. He is as good as dead to them and he thinks his mother is glad. "Remember," she used to say, taking him to events because it was expected, "if anybody asks, you're my baby brother. I'm much too young and pretty to be a mother." If he gripped her hand, she pushed him away, and Lance was powerless because he was too little to live on his own. Well, he isn't powerless now.

They have no idea how powerful he has become.

See, Lance alone knows the MegaMall by heart. He was here before Tick Stiles, before the architects and de-signers, before the construction crews. Lance and Nanny lived in their own trailer in the prairie while the Mega-Mall was still in the planning stage. They were parked far away from Isabella's silver bubble because his mother was busy, and he would only get in the way. Once he tried to crawl into his grandfather's lap. Amos pushed him off with a shudder. "Go away! You look like that picture." Lance knows the one. A little boy with golden curls. He just doesn't know what it means. From that day, the old man kept him at arm's length.

Amos never liked him, but he needed him. Lance found out the day Amos handed him the golden shovel and shoved him out the door. It was Groundbreaking Day at the Mega-Mall. As Lance made the first cut in the prairie sand, Amos gloated. "We are partners now." He watched the honey-comb grow; in the inner sanctum he watched the old man, and he knew in his heart that the spirit behind the Mega-Mall was bad.

Then Amos tried to give him a *special job*. "Find

children," he said, "make friends." Grabbing Lance's arm with knotty fingers, he laughed a mad laugh. "Bring them to me."

"I'd rather die." Lance ran away. He was twelve.

Security caught him and brought him back. His mother looked disappointed to see him again, but the old man! His rage rattled Lance all the way down to the heels. *"After all that I put into you . . ."* He tried wheedling. "Money, power. Don't you want—?"

Lance exploded. "I want freedom. I want you to rot and die!" In exchange for this freedom, Lance had to make certain promises. The terms are spelled out like commandments on the document he signed. Keep certain things secret. Don't go here. Don't go there. Tell no one. In exchange for his pledge, Amos turned him loose. Zozzco provided food and supplies. They gave him the handcar.

He was probably too young to be on his own, but scurrying along behind the scenes from the time he turned twelve, he watched the WhirlyFunRide rise at the heart of the MegaMall. He saw artisans putting the last piece into the great glass dome that crowns the biggest shopping center in the known world. He watched the Special Employee Preview ceremonies and the Grand Opening from hiding, which means that he knows about certain things that happened on those days. He was too young to do anything about it, but he thought: *some day.*

Over the years since then Lance has ridden the length and breadth of all the tunnels on his handcar. He has climbed every exit ladder in every sector of the MegaMall. The tools and equipment Zozzco provided have been put to good use, although Lance will never say how. Work-men don't notice when bits of material go missing, so Lance has fortified his quarters and passed on materials to the night children.

The people in charge won't know that the food and supplies Lance argued for are really for the night children, like so much of what he does. Regular shipments arrive at the designated spot. Lance buzzes from sector to sector, leaving cartons of food for the gangs to "find."

The people in charge can't possibly guess how far Lance has traveled or how much he knows. They don't speak, and if they did, he wouldn't tell them any more than he tells you. He doesn't cause trouble. He doesn't protest. In fact, they don't see Lance any more— not even a glimpse.

Alone in the MegaMall, silent and better than invis-ible, Lance is the ultimate insider. He alone knows the size and shape of the territory. Although he steers clear of for-bidden places, Lance has been through every sector in the growing MegaMall.

More important, Lance knows the night children. All of them.

There are more gangs in the MegaMall than Tick can guess. Because the lives of the night children are lived in secret, they keep to themselves. The growing honeycomb of galleries and courtyards and plazas that makes up the MegaMall is so vast that at night the children can roam freely without ever crossing paths. Or they could until Burt came. From the day the big lout and his posse blun-dered into the mall, Lance knew they meant trouble. A born bully, burly Burt was too lazy to find a new sector for his Dingos to colonize. He wanted to set up housekeeping where he landed, in the Romanesque Sector of the Mega-Mall, never mind who lived there, no matter what.

Burt thought he could drive Tick and the Castertown Crazies out of the MegaMall, but he was wrong. It began with petty skirmishes— safe enough, until the mess over the girl. Woolly-headed Burt is a captive now. Worse. He stampeded Tick into that foolish, gallant rescue attempt. If Amos didn't know about the night children, he knows now.

Now they are all at risk.

There is a flurry of activity in the Dark Hall. Something bad is about to come down.

Lance has work to do.

People to reach. Over the years, he has been in all the places the many tribes of night children have set up housekeeping. He's slept in their hideouts and eaten in front of their underground fires. Only Lance knows for sure where in the mall night children are living; only Lance has visited them in far-flung sectors, listening to their troubles and bringing back whatever they need— tools for the builders, splints and bandages for the ones who get hurt and medicine for children who are sick. They all love Lance. When he gets up from their secret campfires and turns to go they try to follow him, but for their safety, he can't allow it.

He likes these children, but they can't be friends. Lance keeps to himself for their own protection. This is why he chooses not to talk. Let slip any of the things he knows about this place and the people who control it, and kids will start exploring where they aren't supposed to go.

Lance knows better than anyone that there's nothing more dangerous than a bunch of children running scared. There's no telling what Amos will do to children careless enough to get caught. Lance spends his days and nights here preventing it.

This is why Lance says nothing to anybody, but helps where he can. This is why, when he helps you, he disappears before you can say thanks. Sometimes you don't even know he is leaving. You turn around and Lance is gone. In his time, he's made several last-minute rescues, which he did for Jule. Tonight he came into the tunnel too late to save two: Doakie. Burt. Two more rescues to mastermind. For years he's helped the night children stay under cover, off-camera, far from Security, out of sight.

For years they've managed, but Lance is up against it now.

This is what brings the Loner into the forbidden area he agreed never to enter. Oh, yes he has kept his side of the agreement. Until now. Tonight he overheard certain things. To win his freedom, Lance made many promises, but he never promised not to explore.

How could Amos know that in his travels Lance discovered the hidden river that runs deep under the Mega-Mall, or that he built a boat and followed it to its source? That he found water rolling out of the earth in an underground cavern far below the Dark Hall? Who in Zozzco could guess what Lance has been doing, or how much he knows?

The Zozzpeople think the river is their secret, but they're wrong. They don't know that the grotto under the Dark Hall is a giant echo chamber, either, or that from his hideout on the riverbank, Lance hears everything. They don't think about the river at all, except to be sure that technicians keep emptying barrels of tranquilizers into the water that flows out of the MegaMall and on and on for miles, into downtown Castertown.

They'll never guess that unseen and unheard, Lance lingers for hours at the head of the hidden river, with his boat moored underneath the Dark Hall. How could they know that in the grotto, everything said in the Great Room above comes through loud and clear?

He heard them scheming. *They're poisoning the town!*

This is what brings him into forbidden territory to-night. He entered the secret precincts with the master key: the extra protection he slipped into his pocket the day they set him free. He is inside the deserted Communications Center, sitting at the Universal Console. He is trying to figure out what to do.

As agreed, he does not cause trouble, or he hasn't.

Now everything has changed. Tonight he heard Amos and his chief of Security pacing, arguing. Then Amos boomed in a voice that filled the Dark Hall and rocked the cavern below: "ROUND UP ALL CHILDREN. FIND THE LITTLE BRUTES!"

Amos has ordered a Security sweep.

Lance has to warn the night children.

All of them.

Only Lance knows how.

The responsibility is tremendous.

But he has the means.

The trouble now is that all the parts of Lance's life are

in the middle of a personal war. There are the promises he made. There are his loyalties. Whether or not she likes you, your mother is your mother.

There is as well the strange, sad loneliness that links him to the hideous old man, who can't bear the fact that Lance looks like Amos, but handsome. Unscarred. The hint of that likeness underneath his grotesque lumps and disfiguring scabs.

Lance the Loner has lived free for years. He is up against it now.

Right now his loyalties are pulling him eight ways to Sunday but looking at Lance in his ski mask and his neat camo, you'd never know. He is very good at hiding what he feels. He learned from the best. His mother taught him every time she shook off his hand or pushed him away, beginning when he was very small. To keep his dignity, he had to pretend this didn't hurt. He was an expert even before he put on the mask.

What he is feeling right now is anxious and a little scared, but he keeps his head high and his shoulders squared. Inside, he is shaking. Can he do this? How? What will happen to his world if he does?

So far in his life in the MegaMall, Lance has done as told. Agreed. After all, obedience is one of the conditions of his freedom, but the forces in the Dark Hall— *his people*— are planning something unspeakable, and this is Lance's dirty secret. Like Isabella Zozz and the terrible Amos, he is responsible for everything they do. Tonight he heard them talking. Honor or no honor, loyalty or no loyalty, pledges or not, he can't let it go on.

It's time to act.

He will, of course, but what will become of everybody then?

There are places Lance is not supposed to go under any circumstances, and this is one.

There are also things Lance is pledged not to do.

What Lance is doing now, for instance, is absolutely forbidden. It was agreed along with a lot of other things when the powerful Zozz family let him separate from them and walk free.

This is Lance the Loner, considering.

Do not ask Lance what he's going to do. If he doesn't know, he won't tell you.

If he knows, he will definitely not tell you. He won't tell you anything.

It all depends on how this next part comes down.

Like Lance, you will have to wait.

TWENTY-ONE

THEY HAVE BEEN PADDLING upstream for what seems like forever. Then with a thud, Tick's raft noses into a dock.

All his breath rushes out. "We're here."

Jule whispers, "What are we going to do?"

For a long minute Tick plays his flashlight on the ceiling of the grotto here at the head of the hidden river, considering. The place is cavernous. The ceiling arches far above. Finally he answers, "Wait."

Jule is half-crazy with impatience. Standing, she hisses, "We can't just sit here and wait!"

He does what he has to; roughly, he pulls her down. "Yes we can. Until the others come."

She can't hold still. "Do something!"

"Not until we know what to do."

They are directly under the Dark Hall. The river comes rushing out of a cavernous hole in the earth. The current's strong. With an effort, Tick has pulled his raft out of the mainstream and into a little backwater carved into the rock. It's been a long, hard trip from the Hall of Beauty, with Tick's little flotilla rowing against the current all the way.

By the time they set out on this expedition, all his Crazies were assembled; there are others coming, but he hasn't told Jule.

Together, the Crazies swarmed down the well in the Hall of Beauty, hard on Mag's heels. They went through the hatch at the bottom and down the ladder to the banks of the hidden river, handing along the light equipment and lowering the rest on ropes. They were still coming long after Tick and Jule got on the first raft and pushed off from shore. On the riverbank far below the fountain in the Hall of Beauty, Jule saw kids she knows and kids she wishes she didn't know launching their boats. They are still coming in.

One by one, the other rafts emerge from the flow and nose in, nudging the dock like so many whales. Tick steps up, onto the dock. The others move to follow but he raises his hand like a school crossing guard. "There are more people coming," he says. "Wait for the rest."

Grumbling, they settle back. Tick leaves redheaded Mag posted on the dock, squinting into the dimness like an angry troll. Behind her, the great river stretches. With Willie and James, she will guide the stragglers in to the dock, where they will wait for Tick's signal. Until it comes, it is their job to stand watch.

"OK," he says, holding out a hand to Jule.

Ignoring it, she scrambles onto the dock. "Now?"

"Now."

She follows Tick onto the narrow bank. Bolted to the wall of the cavern beyond the dock is a ladder leading up. Tick sweeps it with his light. Overhead the ladder fits neatly into a chute cut out of solid rock, leading up into

Zozzco's secret places. At the bottom, Tick stands with one hand on the first rung.

Jule is impatient; they have been still for much too long. "All right. Let's go."

Tick shakes his head. "Not yet."

Behind them, boys and girls are still coming on rafts and in kayaks and aluminum canoes, gliding in without making a sound. Somebody gasps. It's the Dingo tribe.

Jule is outraged. "The Dingos!"

"Quiet."

She is sputtering. "But we can't let them . . ."

Tick doesn't respond. On the dock, Mag raises her arm. He raises his like a starter's flag.

"You knew she was bringing the—"

"I said, *quiet*." Tick and Mag exchange nods. They are working together now.

Whether or not she wants to see it, Jule knows that Tick is right. Although the Dingos and Crazies thought they were enemies, they are pulling together here. Emergencies make strange bedfellows. When the call went out on cell phones and pagers, children in both tribes dropped whatever they were doing and came. As Tick's instructions scrolled up the screens of cells and BlackBerries, the Castertown Crazies and the Dingos forgot their differences and moved out together, collecting supplies. From the food courts, from the music and video galleries and the amusement plaza, from wherever they were roving, the Castertown Crazies and the Dingos come, carrying flare guns and baseball bats, jackknives and starter's pistols, slingshots and sparklers, whatever they think is needed for what happens next.

On their way to the hidden river, the tribes raided the Sporting Goods gallery and took things, something Tick's night children have never done before. Under pressure, they broke in and they stole. The rules just changed. This is an emergency. They had no choice. Along with the items on Tick's list they have brought fireworks and megaphones, everything they could think of and everything that came to hand. Badminton nets, bows and arrows, pellet guns, in case . . .

In case of what?

Nobody knows.

They'll know soon enough, and most of them are afraid.

Whatever happens, the Crazies and the Dingo tribe are working together now. The night children sit together without moving, waiting for the signal.

Jule is waiting too.

Tick just isn't ready to give it yet.

He stands with that hand on the ladder. Listening.

The suspense is worse than whatever they have to fight, Jule thinks. When you hate waiting, the worst thing anybody can do to you is make you wait. Living with the Castertown Crazies, she thought she had learned how to be a team player, but Jule is used to being her own boss. Waiting is hard for her. It always has been.

How can they just sit here, with poor little Doakie trapped up there in the Dark Hall? She doesn't care about Burt Arno but she does care about Doakie, and who knows how many others Zozzco has trapped? They have to hurry! Can't he see it? Everything is at risk and yet, Tick waits. He is listening.

The only sound in the giant echo chamber is the whistle of air in the stone chute leading up. If there was anybody tramping around up there in the Dark Hall, you'd never know it. If Mag thought she heard Burt shouting for help when she came running to Tick, he isn't shouting now. There are no footsteps vibrating overhead and there are no voices. If she hears anything, it's the sound of nothing happening.

Jule wheels, studying the cross little redhead. For all she knows, Mag lied to get them all here. She mutters to Tick, "What if this is a Dingo trap?"

"Don't."

"What if Mag got us down here to get even?"

"I said, don't."

Furious, she clenches her teeth and waits. It's killing her. As far as she can tell, the Dark Hall is empty now. If they have Doakie up there somewhere, whoever *they* are, if they really do have Burt in their clutches, if indeed they have prisoners— Mom? Dad?— you'd never know it. Everything is still.

"Come on," she murmurs. "What's keeping you?"

Silent, Tick looks at his watch.

Jule is one of those people who doesn't need a watch to know what time it is. It's near dawn. Too near dawn, she realizes, if they're going to do this before sunup and get back to the hideout before the morning cleaning crews come in. She jogs his arm. "It's getting late!"

Instead of responding, he blinks, and new to the life as she is, Jule understands that Tick has brought them here without a plan.

"What's the matter, Tick? Are you scared?"

"No."

"Then go!" All they have to do is start up that ladder. "Let's go up and get this over with!"

"Not until I'm sure."

"Sure of what." She is getting angry. "Sure of *what*?"

"Sure that it's safe. I can't let anybody get hurt."

"Don't worry. I'll be careful."

Tick says in a harsh whisper, "You're not the only person I have to think about."

At his side now, she grabs the ladder. "Let's go!"

"I have to think."

"Well, I don't!"

"That's your whole problem," Tick says sharply. It's like a smack in the face.

Instead of making her think, it makes her mad.

Behind them in the boats, boys and girls shift impatiently, but nobody speaks. For this many people, they are amazingly silent. Even Jiggy and Nance are quiet, for now. For a bunch of oddly assorted would-be enemies, the high level of self-control is amazing. Nobody whispers. Nobody giggles. Nobody moves except Jule, whose fingers and toes are curling as though she's already climbing; everything in her is rushing ahead.

Most people are holding their breath.

But Jule is new to night in the MegaMall. She hasn't spent her life running and hiding like the others. She has been on the WhirlyFunRide more times than any person in the MegaMall, boy, girl or adult, and she's not afraid of anything. She's not! Before Tick can stop her, she starts to climb.

"Girl, what are you *doing*?"

"I'm going up."

TWENTY-TWO

AT THE TOP OF the ladder, Jule comes out into a stupendous stillness. Nobody speaks. Nothing moves. The Dark Hall is as bleak and featureless as a black star.

She has come up in the Great Room at its center. What little light there is comes from overhead lights marking the point where the vaulted ceiling gives way to a glistening black glass dome. The shadows are so deep that she can see almost nothing. She can't hear anything. Trembling, she sprawls on the gleaming onyx floor and waits.

Below her, Tick is climbing. She can hear his light footfalls on the ladder as he comes up. Whether or not the leader wanted it, they have begun. Will he pop out of the hole in the floor in a rage, and attack her for going when he told her to wait? Can she start exploring or will she end up fighting Tick just to keep him from forcing her back down the ladder? She doesn't know.

Now that she's here, Jule wonders if she moved too fast.

She doesn't know what Tick is going to do. She has no idea what he has planned. She doesn't know whether he intends to scope out the place before they try anything or if he wants to do what she wants to do, which is rush in and rescue Doakie and Burt Arno however. She doesn't even know whether they're strong enough or smart enough to rescue anybody.

She just thinks they need to do something. *Anything* to end the suspense.

Jule is worried about Burt Arno, but not really. She's worried about Doakie, but not as much as she's worried about the other prisoners in the Dark Hall.

Mag says they're going to do something awful to the prisoners. Whoever *They* are. Security? Zozzco? Or does the girl mean somebody else— whatever sinister, nameless power commands the Dark Hall?

Above Jule's head the smoked glass dome pushes against a sky that is just beginning to turn pale. Outside the sun's coming up, but the glass is engineered so that very little light penetrates here. Life in this eerie space unfolds in shadow.

She doesn't know, but she suspects that like the night children, whoever or whatever force drives the Dark Hall sleeps by day and goes about its business after the Mega-Mall closes for the night. This means that the Dark Hall and all its people must be sleeping now. At least she hopes they're sleeping.

She and Tick have come up into the central plaza where the main events take place. Whatever they are.

Rows of black marble benches ring the basalt walls in the circular hall. They are staged in tiers, as though crowds of people assemble here for some ritual Jule has trouble imagining. She doesn't know whether the higher-ups at

Zozzco gather here to watch Aztec rituals complete with sacrifice or to see gladiators in combat or captives fighting lions the way they did in Julius Caesar's day.

Instead of a central fountain like courtyards in the other sectors, the center of the onyx Great Room is marked only by a circle of inlaid gold. Big things happen here at the heart of the Dark Hall, she is sure of it. Something big happens and young as they are, unarmed and unprepared, she and Tick Stiles are here to stop it.

Whatever it is.

The knowledge rips through her like a cold wind and leaves her shivering.

The place is too big. This is all too much.

This is going to be hard.

She wants it to begin. She's afraid to begin. They aren't ready. Tick and his night children have no idea what they're facing or what they'll be called on to do. *Right, Tick,* she thinks, sighing. On a better day, she would stop to apologize. *No wonder you were taking your time.*

Just then Tick slips out of the chute and rolls into position next to her. He isn't angry. Grim as he looks, he manages a grin. "Looks like we made it."

Jule wants to apologize for rushing this but they are beyond that now. She grins right back at him. "We did."

Tick is trying to sound brave, but he finishes with a gulp. "Ready or not."

At first the Dark Hall beyond the circular Great Room seems empty, but there is a spectral uneasiness in the dimness. They hear a rustle in the air. They are not alone. They are aware of slight movement in the corridors leading away from the circular courtyard. Bizarre as it is, on closer inspection the Dark Hall turns out to be laid out like all the other sectors. There are six curved archways visible. Six corridors lead out from the circular Great Room. The nearest ones open on ground floor galleries flanked by storefronts with second-floor balconies above, housing shop after shop, protected by smoked glass ceilings that arch overhead.

Jule whispers, "Why is it so dark in here?"

"He doesn't want anybody to see what's going on," Tick says. He puts a hand on her wrist, holding her in place. "Shhh."

For a moment, everything is still.

Now that she's used to the profound silence, Jule hears people breathing. Bodies stirring as people roll over in their sleep. Her mind rushes ahead. Are there tribes of grownups living in the MegaMall? Do they hide out here in the Dark Hall, sleeping in the stores? Are the glass-and-neon displays in the gallery nearest them really ordinary shops or do the night children have friends in the Dark Hall, kindred souls living here? She doesn't know.

After a moment, Tick whispers, "Let's go."

Inching along on their bellies, she and Tick head for the archway. As they approach the gallery she sees that there are no shuttered storefronts in this hallway, at least not the usual kinds. There are metal grilles, all right, the kind of grillework that rolls down at night to protect every storefront in the mall, but behind the grilles . . .

They advance, worming along— who *knows* what alarms will go off if they stand? Odd, Jule thinks. There are no surveillcams here.

After what seems like hours, they reach the gallery and roll inside. Blinking into the dimness, they see . . .

All her breath rushes out. "Oh!"

At the same time she hears Tick rumbling from somewhere deep. "My God."

Each grilled front conceals— not a store, exactly, and not an apartment— just something weird. From here it looks as though the enclosures the grilles are protecting aren't stores, they're cells. Oh, the fittings are all there: counters, display cases, registers, signs, but there is something terribly wrong. The spaces designed to look like stores really are cells. They are laid out like rooms in a dollhouse once you take the roof off to move the family around, with . . .

Not dolls.

Jule's belly clenches. She hopes against hope that those are store dummies she sees sleeping in the other cells, lying on sofas and in beds and reclining chairs. She doesn't know. "Tick," she whispers, "do you think . . ."

They hear a sneeze.

"Prisoners." His voice is so ragged that it scares her.

"It can't be."

"We have to make sure."

Prisoners. Gulping, Jule follows as Tick gets up and darts toward the first storefront. She can't help hoping that maybe the figures in the windows and the figures inside are really store dummies after all, dressed up animatronics, a quaint display like one at Disney World. She and Tick are, after all, only two kids with a few more kids waiting for them on the river down below. The night children are smart and they're tough, but even if all the

Crazies and Dingos come up the ladder together at this very moment, what could they do? They are no army. They're just kids.

If there are real people trapped behind all these steel gratings, and the prisoners have been put here by Zozzco or whatever power governs the Dark Hall, all the children in the universe may not be strong enough to fight and win and get them out.

Together, Jule and Tick advance.

The first storefront is fixed up like an old-fashioned pharmacy, with pill dispensers and products and miniature scales and a marble counter and massed bottles filled with colored liquids in gleaming display cases. A perfect old-fashioned shop. At first glance the shop looks empty but as Tick and Jule peer in, a pale, skeletal figure in a white coat totters out from behind the counter and hisses, "Go back. Hurry. Hurry," he pleads. "You can't stay here!"

So it's true. Jule whispers, "What are we going to do?"

The face Tick turns to her now is drawn and tortured. "Save them, I guess."

"But how?"

"Try." Tick pushes the point of his knife on the lock that secures the grille.

"No. Quiet. Don't," the pale pharmacist squeaks in a mad attempt to whisper and warn them at the same time. "Don't, or you'll bring them."

"We came to help you."

"Help yourselves," the old man says, "You can't."

"We have to try."

From outside the gallery comes the sound of many feet, coming from far away.

"They're coming, now, hide!" The captive pharmacist swells up with the effort. The warning comes out in a whoosh. "Get down!"

In a flash Tick drops like a marine dodging a shell.

"Hurry!"

As Jule stands, transfixed and blinking, two things happen.

First, a little storm of desperate whispers begins in the gallery as pale, thin people imprisoned in dozens of stores behind dozens of other grilles become aware that there are outsiders here in the gallery. The captives whisper on and on, warning the two intruders to go somewhere else, anywhere else, before they get themselves and all the prisoners in trouble.

Unless the people trapped in these stores are begging Tick and Jule to break them out. They are so upset that it's hard to know. What they do know is that these trapped adults in their silly costumes are Amos Zozz's toys.

Tick hisses at Jule, "Get down."

But something else is happening, something so big that it freezes Jule in her tracks. A rush of laughter and loud voices fills the courtyard, preceded by the sound of drumming feet and the hum of fat rubber tires. Under the archway leading in from the far gallery, there is a parade forming up. Transfixed, she watches Zozzpeople on massed rolling chairs with flashing headlights and flying banners roll into position.

Meanwhile, above the golden ring that marks the center of the Dark Hall, blinding searchlights come to life, beginning a slow sweep of the giant circular room.

Gasping, Jule whirls.

Something big is about to begin.

She turns to Tick. *"What?"*

"I think it's what we came here to stop."

The chairs part and Security streams in. Dozens of troops with their cockroach visors pulled down thud into the arena and form a little honor guard.

Next the parade of vehicles rolls in, fanning out to make a little avenue for . . . Jule cranes to see. Something big is coming, a barge or a parade float carrying a . . . What? She isn't sure. She is crazy to see!

"Down," the ancient pharmacist whispers urgently. "Down."

Tick tugs at her ankle. "Get down!"

Riveted, Jule watches as spotlights play on the onyx courtyard. The honor guard of Security troops turns to face the far gallery but the roving spotlights sweep on, toward the spot where Jule Devereaux is still standing, bright as day.

Tick grabs her ankle. "Get down."

And all the unknown prisoners trapped behind the storefronts whisper as one, "Get down!"

Unused as she is to following orders, Jule doesn't argue. She drops like a stone onto the floor.

The prisoners draw in a single breath. It rushes out in a warning, as though they can blow Jule and Tick out of the path of the moving spotlights: "Hide!"

Fate provides a distraction. Trumpeters play the Zozzco jingle, a little fanfare. Everybody in the place turns to face the gallery directly opposite. For the moment, their backs are to the gallery where the night children shrink.

Tick whispers, "Now."

Clinging to the onyx floor, the two wriggle out into the courtyard. Like night fighters in a secret army, they roll under one of the black marble benches that ring the Dark Hall.

As they do so, a hush falls on the Great Room.

Then a cheer goes up in the great black courtyard as the honor guard of Security troops falls back and the Zozzco executives' golf carts roll into position to make a little avenue for the approaching barge or parade float that carries . . . their leader? The monster that governs the Dark Hall? What?

Lined with flowers and trimmed with gold, magnificent with its golden double Zs and its black satin draperies, the ceremonial float rolls in, carrying a black straight chair planted like a throne on the little platform at dead center. Sitting in the straight chair is a figure that Jule can not make out, because she is blinded by the light. Whoever it is, it's only a silhouette to her. Then the rolling mountain of black satin and gold enters the ring defined by the gold circle in the onyx floor and stops.

The roving spotlights go out.

A single strong light plays on the float and fixes on the figure in the austere straight chair.

After a pause, the figure gestures and one of his black-suited lackeys presents a microphone. The light narrows to a pin spot on his face. Tick elbows Jule and she grunts. *It's him.* Where his people are dressed in business suits or Security uniforms, this person . . . no, this *personage* is tall in gold platform boots and gorgeous in a sweeping black robe.

Old, he is incredibly old. His head shines like a piece of ivory polished to a high gloss. A mystery, until Jule sees that his entire head is covered in gleaming platinum. The true face of the *personage* is protected by a handsome mask. The beautiful beaten metal face is as stern and cruel as an Aztec idol's. The platinum top of the head is flawless and perfectly rounded, bare as a naked skull. Stringy as its body is, the figure looks strong and stern and in this setting, extremely powerful.

The air in the courtyard buzzes and sizzles. "Z . . . zzz . . . zzz . . . z . . ." It sounds like a thousand hornets worshiping something bigger than they are. "Z . . . zzz . . . zzz . . . z . . ."

"Shut up!" The big voice crackles in all the loudspeakers.

As one, the dozens of uniformed followers clap their foreheads, roaring, "Zozz!"

Jule's heart stumbles. "Is that . . ."

With a touch on the arm, Tick silences her.

The Zozzpeople applaud until their leader raises his hand, shouting in a voice loud enough to fill the hall. "Stop!"

His people fall silent too.

"Now. We have work to do." He orders, "Bring Isabella."

A hundred voices rise, "Isabella . . . Isabella . . . bella . . . ella . . ." Then a hundred people fall silent and wait.

The figure in the black robe is frighteningly still. He is like a statue of a king, waiting. Then, loud enough to short out the speakers for several seconds, he shouts, "Isabella!"

There is a clatter in the far corridor, the sound of someone running in tremendously high heels. Gasping and disheveled in her once-perfect white suit, the woman Jule knows only from the portrait in Town Hall rushes to the base of the platform, crying, "Yes, Father. Yes!" So much for the haughty Isabella Zozz. She's just as scared of their leader as everybody else.

Now the man in flowing black pushes back the chair and stands. He is tall. No, he is tremendous. Towering over everybody in the courtyard, the figure in the platinum mask commands, "Bring out the new prisoners."

It is Amos Zozz.

TWENTY-THREE

IT IS SOME TIME later.

Bent over the console in the Communications Center in Zozzco headquarters, Lance is watching the proceedings in the Dark Hall. They have been going on for much too long. Why has the old man turned this day into a call to judgment? Why is the judging so personal, and why is the old man so cruel?

Lance watches the march of the prisoners— a sad procession of people who didn't deserve to be at the mercy of Amos Zozz. Some, he remembers from the early days. They are the builders and designers Amos took prisoner; the powerful billionaire keeps them captive in the drafting gallery, working away on— what? Lance knows they spend their days chained to their drawing boards, working on a secret project for the old man.

Embittered old Amos has always been a spoiler. Lance remembers what evil joy he took in moving people around like pieces on the chessboard back when Lance was small. Cackling, the old man patted his round satin bed. "Come play, boy. Look. Isn't this wonderful?"

"No, it's awful!"

"Come back," Amos cried. "Some day all this will be yours."

"Well, I don't want it!" Sobbing, Lance fled.

The old man shouted after him; the words lashed at his ankles, cutting him to the bone. "Well, what are you going to do about it?"

What can I do? he thought at the time— he was eight! Shuddering, he retreated. *Nothing,* he thought emptily. He did what he could at the time. He separated. He grew.

Now Lance the Loner says in a strong, loud voice, "Yet."

Lance knew in his bones that this day was coming sooner or later. He just didn't expect it to come so soon.

Neither did Amos, he sees, which may give Lance the advantage.

Look at the old man standing up there in the mask of beaten platinum he puts on when he meets the public, imposing in the black cape and the long black robe. See the elevated boots, crafted especially to make him look taller than he really is. Amos has put on the face he wants his people to see, which is nothing like his real face, Lance knows all too well. He is glorying in the odd beauty the mask and the fittings give him. He is glorying in the power.

Like the pharaoh of a long-dead civilization, Amos makes his prisoners kneel at the foot of the dais. "Some of you," he says in a big voice, "will be useful as we enter Phase Two, and the rest of you . . ."

During the pause that follows, the weak ones weep and the strong ones groan.

Twirling his bony fingers, Amos quiets the group like a director at an audition. "The rest of you will have to prove yourselves! I decide," he shouts.

The silence that follows is terrible.

Lance grinds his teeth. *This is even worse than I thought.* If he'd stayed above ground, if he'd put on the uniform and lived in company headquarters, could he have prevented this? Or would he be propped up in one of Amos's commercial display cases, dressed as a shoemaker? Would he have ended up behind bars in the deepest dungeon in the Dark Hall? Lance doesn't know. He only knows that for the longest time, he was too young to do anything about all this, except walk away. But now . . .

Sick down to the toes of his thick army boots, Lance understands that the old man has brought all these people— including the uniformed Zozzpeople in the audience, who think they are here to watch— to judgment. Oh, he'll make a show of it, Amos loves to make people suffer for his own entertainment, but there is something much more sinister going on.

He is rushing into the mysterious Phase Two.

"Prisoners of the Dark Hall," Amos bellows. "Convince me you are worthy!"

As Lance watches, the willful tycoon summons his prisoners to the platform, one by one. They are carefully kept, these Zozz prisoners, combed and elaborately dressed, like dolls refurbished to fit into a playhouse owned by a large, spoiled child. Some, Amos keeps because they are useful, and the others . . . It's hard to say.

As the prisoners step up on the dais he says to them, one after another, "Show me what you've got!"

They are all desperate to prove themselves. In the parade to judgment the architects and designers come first. The architects carry miniature scale models of new sectors, and designers present sketches and blueprints for improvements to come. As the prisoners keep coming Lance recognizes some of Castertown's missing councilmen, the ones who voted against the MegaMall. Trusted Zozzco employees follow— executives who, Lance had been told, had resigned. He sees captive chefs come in flourishing their best dishes and he sees shop owners; he sees the athletes and models who serve as ornaments in the old man's palatial apartments simply because they're beautiful. One by one they step up to judgment by Amos Zozz.

These are followed by a sad procession of shoppers foolish enough to max out their credit cards while still on the premises. Some of the shoppers, Amos uses as living displays in his shopping dioramas; pale and miserable, they look weary in their period costumes, from frilly nineteenth-century French outfits and wigs to early pioneer garb, dressed up because better than anything, Amos loves to control. Some are his personal servants. The luckier debtors, Amos has turned into entertainers or models in the midnight fashion shows at which he sits like a king, handsome in his splendid platinum mask.

Lance watches as the MegaMall captives step up on the dais. They give speeches or show paintings and blueprints or perform dramatic monologs or do frantic tap dances in an attempt to demonstrate their worth.

There is an excruciating silence when they're done.

Did they please Amos? Does anybody? What happens to the ones who fail?

Lance leans forward as Amos delivers the verdict: "OK."

Or, more often: "I'm tired of you!" That imperious wave. "Take him away."

The old man sends his captives, his *creatures* to the right or to his left, according to whether they are to stay in the Castertown MegaMall or be disposed of. A third group huddles in the enclosure nearest the platform.

They are the chosen. Earmarked for Phase Two. Most of the builders, designers and decorators have been herded into the enclosure, where Security guards them behind velvet ropes.

The others have a harder time. In the hour that Lance has been watching, a handful of the old man's captive storekeepers and clothing models have gotten the OK. When this is over, Lance supposes, the approved ones will go back to their environments. Correction. Cells.

What happens to the rest? In a hastily erected corral to the left of Amos Zozz, a growing crowd of the old man's discarded playthings waits, muttering. He is like an angry child, ready to destroy anything that displeases him. If they're thinking to escape, they can forget it. All of Mega-Mall Security is lined up here, closing the circle.

Finally the billionaire founder and owner of the Caster-town MegaMall, the wealthy and terrifying Amos Zozz, tires of the activity. It is not enough to own the people here. He is bored. Amos Zozz is totally bored!

Disgusted, he shouts, "That's enough for now. And after the break . . ." He finishes with an ugly laugh. "Just you wait."

The unexamined prisoners still lined up waiting for

their moment of judgment jostle and fret. What will become of them?

"I said, that's enough! Take them away!" With an imperious wave, Amos shouts, "I'm sick of you."

The words hit Lance in the stomach like a sack of rocks. He doesn't know how this will end, only that it will end badly. There is a hush in the Dark Hall. Then Amos looks up. It is almost as though he is talking directly into the surveill camera. No. As if he is talking directly to Lance.

"I'm sick of you too."

Then he turns to his employees, the loyal Zozzpeople, saying in that harsh, dry voice that carries to the ends of the Dark Hall. "I'm sick of you all!"

Their moan grows like a whirlwind. "Ooooh, nooooo."

Amos says directly to the camera, "What am I going to do with you?"

Lance gulps. He knows better, but Amos is talking in that odd, pointed way that Lance knows all too well.

Then Amos twirls his fingers as though none of this has happened and food comes. Late at night or early in the morning as it is, roasts come in on silver salvers and Yorkshire pudding comes on platters and steamed plum puddings come and coffee in great gold samovars comes. Lackeys lay out a banquet table and Amos Zozz steps down and takes the great chair at the head of the table. On the mogul's right sits his daughter, Isabella Zozz. Smug, because without Lance here, she is second in command. Although he saw overdressed Isabella rush into the Great Room all disheveled and distracted when this show began, her hair is once again perfect.

Every fingernail glitters like steel. The sleek white suit and the golden wedge heels and the gold-and-diamond Zozzco emblem hanging at the cold but beautiful Isabella's throat make her stand out like a white tiger among all the scared, dutiful Zozzco executives buzzing around her in their black suits.

Isabella smiles at the camera— does she know Lance is here? Sweet-looking face for once. In spite of everything she has done. Something big and sad jumps in Lance's throat.

Amos says, "Isabella."

"Yes, Father."

An odd, new sound comes out of Amos Zozz. It is an ominous laugh. "Wait'll you get a load of my next project."

Knowing the old man, Lance shudders to think. He clenches his fists. *You could stop him if you wanted to.*

The lines in the platinum mask pull together in an evil leer. "You're gonna love it."

You can't!

The people in the Great Room won't hear what he hisses into Isabella's ear but she hears, and sitting in the Communications Center, Lance hears. Spit flies around inside the platinum mask as Amos whispers, "The children."

The children! Lance strains forward, willing her: *Lady, do something!*

The dry whisper continues. "Time to deal with the children."

Startled, Isabella blinks. For a second, the beautiful, vain woman Lance knows too well to admire, ponders. She is deciding whether or not Amos is crazy. She's deciding whether it's time to make that grab for power. Many things hang in the balance.

Lance fumes. *Aren't you going to do anything?*

Instead, Isabella turns to her father, fawning with a deceitful smile. Her next words bring Lance to his feet. "How positively divine."

Lance pounds the console. *No!* He has come to a decision.

With the flip of a switch, Lance the Loner diverts audio transmission from the Dark Hall sector into the system that serves the entire MegaMall. Part One. All he has to do is trip the switch. Where he has lived in the tunnels for years, observing without the power to change what goes on here, everything just changed. Where he thought moving out kept him from being responsible for what goes on here, it's not that easy. Lance has changed. He is preparing to act.

One-way streets are the easiest traveled, Lance tells himself, and is not sure what that means.

What he does next has to be done quickly. It's getting late. Cleaning crews on the early morning shift will be finishing up in all the shopping sectors. The first shuttles of the day from Castertown and from the MegaMall Airport are preparing to bring hundreds of retail clerks to the stores, cooks and wait-people to the many restaurants, the daytime security guards to replace the sinister night shift.

Masses of earlybird shoppers are lined up at the entrances, all hoping to be first in the Castertown MegaMall. Soon the stores in all the galleries will be filled with workers. Soon, Lance knows, shoppers will fan out in every courtyard and every corridor. There will be thousands of people here in the MegaMall.

In ordinary circumstances, this might be a bad thing for Lance, who spends his daytime hours in the MegaMall avoiding outsiders. He prefers to stay hidden, but given what's going on right now, having people by the thousands stalking the MegaMall along with him is a good thing. In an odd way, it fits in with his plan.

Therefore, Lance prerecords two short messages. This is Part Two. They will go mallwide when it's time.

Then he presets the amplifying system to pipe his announcements into every sector at specific times— one ten minutes from now, while the galleries and tunnels are empty of everyone but stray night children and the cleanup crews, and the second thirty minutes from now, when the shoppers are scheduled to start coming in.

Once this is done, Lance sets a third timer. This one activates the mallwide sound system. Then he picks up the remote.

When he triggers the sound system, everyone in the old man's vast shopping empire will hear what's going on in the Dark Hall.

Just when he should be leaving, Lance turns back to the banks of screens. He spends a long minute studying Isabella Zozz in close-up. Beautiful, really. In spite of that flash of sweetness, greedy and cold. Too loyal to Amos to do anything but stand by while he has his way. It has paid off for her. Look at the gold stripes on her sleeve. Zozzco second in command. *Is it worth it, really?*

"Oh, Mother," he rumbles in a voice rusty from disuse. "Get over yourself."

Then with a shrug, he turns his back on the polished image of Isabella Zozz and closes the door on the Communications Center for good. He locks it and walks away. It doesn't take long to lift the grate in the marble floor in the management sector. Where he spent a long time considering what to do next, Lance is quick and decisive now. Bypassing the ladder, he grabs the fireman's pole and slides down to the loading dock where his tram is parked.

He sets the gauges and kicks it into *high*.

From here, he will move fast.

TWENTY-FOUR

THE CHANGING LIGHT ON the onyx floor tells Tick and Jule that far above the smoked glass dome above the Great Room, the sun is climbing in the sky. From where they are lying, flat on their bellies on the onyx floor of the circular Great Room, they watch legs and shuffling feet go by as the tycoon's last prisoners advance to the dais on the forced march to judgment. Faces are harder to see, although they are trying.

They've been lying here for so long that the cold bites to the bone, leaving them stiff and shivering. Could they move if they had to? Stand up? Run? They don't know. The crowd is so thick that the night children can't see much of the captives, but they can hear them, and— the voices!

The old man's prisoners sound so much like friends, like *relatives* that it's hard to keep from yelling, "Hang on, we came to help!" How, exactly, is a big question. Huddled under the bench, Jule sobs without making a sound. Deep in shadow though they are, she can see tears running down Tick's face.

The sad procession drags on until finally even Amos tires of it.

"Enough," he shouts. Confetti overflows the giant shredder his hulking vice presidents hoisted onto the platform before the trials began. For what seems like forever he examined blueprints and sketches. He studied designs and business plans produced by prisoners commanded to prove their worth. They'll do anything to earn a ticket to Phase Two, even though Amos alone knows what Phase Two really means.

Survival, Tick supposes.

Jule wonders: What does he do with his playthings when he tires of them?

Disgusted, Amos has fed most of the prisoners' offerings to his hungry shredder, casting the bearers aside without caring where they fell. What if he shreds unwanted prisoners too? "Enough," he shouts again.

Still they come.

Amos roars, "I said, enough!"

The few remaining are so terrified that they flood the dais, tap dancers and ballerinas and clowns alike, frantically doing the buck-and-wing, wild pirouettes and mad cartwheels, anything to make him choose them.

"Stop that! I'm sick of you!" At a wave of his hand, helmeted guards remove the last of them.

"Now," Amos says in a voice big enough to fill the Great Room. "On to the next thing."

On the cold onyx floor under a cold stone bench, Jule and Tick shiver, waiting. The rejected prisoners cower, waiting. Zozzco officials and Security anxiously await orders.

The atmosphere in the Dark Hall is thick with despair.

Just when they are all about to die of waiting, Amos says so loud that even the senior vice presidents tremble, "The surprise!"

Jule thinks the floor is shaking, but she's shivering too hard to be sure.

"Out with the old," Amos Zozz begins.

Jule grabs Tick's wrist. They exchange looks. *What are we going to do?* Two kids, in the presence of all this power.

On the platform, Amos finishes, "In with the new!"

His Zozzpeople cheer.

Tick says through his teeth, "Try to save them, I suppose."

And for the first time ever, Jule Devereaux has to admit, "We can't do it alone."

Sadly, Tick mouths the word: *No.*

"Now!!!" The next thing Amos says stops their hearts. "You may not know it, but there are wild children in the MegaMall, running like rats in a maze."

"Oooooh," the Zozzpeople moan obediently. "Nooooo."

Amos goes on in a dry, hard voice. "Last week they were foolish enough to show themselves."

"Oooooh, nooooo!"

"And Security let them get away! Don't worry," the old man says scornfully. "You'll pay."

Jule has her ear to the floor, listening. She pokes Tick: *Do you hear it too?*

The Zozzco lament turns into a long groan. "Ooooooh, noooooo!"

Tick nods. Something big is rolling in from a long way off. But with his ear to the floor now, he remembers that the Great Room sits over a grotto where his Crazies and the Dingos float, waiting. They can hear this too.

"Filthy children." Amos shakes with disgust. "Running wild!" Then an ugly laugh rattles the platinum mask. "Well, we have them where we want them now."

Tick mutters, "Not all of them." The night children can't fight the Zozzpeople here and now, he sees. They're too young and there are too few, but. But! Bobbing in the grotto, the children in Tick's little flotilla are hearing this as clearly as he and Jule do. Every word that Amos says. Everything! Thinking fast, he texts a note to his main men:

RIDE RVR 2 CASTRTWN. BRING HELP.

The kids waiting in the underground river may not be their last hope, exactly, but it's close.

"Wild *children*." The old man's masked head rattles with a sinister laugh. "Rampaging and getting in the way. Hating us the way you did . . ."

Tick looks at Jule. *What is this?*

"Teasing us," Amos says wildly. "When all we wanted was to be friends! Locking us up in their dollhouse and leaving us to the mercy of a pack of . . ."

Jule looks at Tick. *Has he gone crazy?* Tick shrugs.

Up on the dais, the old man coughs up grief like a hairball. "Monsters, and they thought they were in control . . ." Moving past the bad, indelible memory that threw his voice out of control for a minute there, he draws himself up as if it never happened. In the mask, he looks eight feet tall. Now Amos goes on in a voice as hard and cold as the platinum mask that covers his entire head. "Well, not any more."

Long pause.

He says in a hard, cold voice, "I am in control of the children now." He finishes with an awful laugh. "And I have *plans* for them."

Tick flinches. Did Willie get his message? Did James? He grits his teeth, trying to beam thoughts to his friends: *Get help.*

Jule nudges him, hissing, "Got to warn them."

Amos says, "And now, the grand surprise. Designers, roll out the prototype!"

Tick mutters through his teeth, "Yes!" Are his main men floating downstream now, he wonders. As told? He tries to move them through sheer force of will. *Go, guys. Go!*

Behind them, great doors open. Something tremendous is being rolled in.

Together, Jule and Tick inch forward on their elbows. It's hard to see much without showing themselves, but there's something oddly familiar about the monumental object pulled up next to the old man's platform.

It's . . .

Brilliantly colored plastic tubes and ladders and Plexi chutes and slides and transparent tunnels and shiny chrome gerbil wheels sit inside an oversized display case on wheels. The beautifully designed creation of plastic and Plexiglas is a familiar object, but with a difference. The difference here is in the scale.

The big plastic-and-metal structure before them is grotesque. Its yards and yards of winding tubes and funnels are sealed inside a glass enclosure bigger than any public aquarium where whales and dolphins swim. The top of the monstrous plastic habitat reaches almost to the smoked glass dome. The thing is big enough to hold everybody in the Great Room of the Dark Hall. In spite of the scale the oversized object is disturbingly familiar.

Tick and Jule and Amos Zozz, who ordered this thing made, and all the Zozzco vice presidents and Security guards and their captives are . . .

They are . . . they are . . .

They are looking at a gigantic Habitrail.

Now the Zozzpeople join the prisoners and Security in muttering and fretting. Is it for the prisoners? For them? Confusion bubbles. Nobody knows.

Amos says in a voice strong enough to split stone, "Behold the MegaTrail!"

The courtyard buzzes as all present gasp and mumble.

"Be warned. This is only the prototype." His big voice gets even bigger. "And this is only the beginning. One day there will be a MegaTrail in every MegaMall in civilization as we know it, and there will be many. And then . . ."

There is a rush of air as everybody gasps. It is followed by complete silence. Everybody in the Dark Hall has stopped breathing.

Then Amos laughs.

The sound is terrible.

He shrieks, "There will be no more children anywhere. No children to ruin our lives. They'll all be safe in my MegaTrails, and . . ." The laughter goes up and up, out of control. Finally the rest comes out in an uncontrollable scream of pain. "Whenever I feel like it, I'll put in the hornets' nests!"

Out of the silence that follows comes the most terrible thing of all as Amos shouts:

"AND THEN THEY'LL KNOW WHAT IT'S LIKE TO BE TRAPPED AND CRYING AND BEGGING TO GET OUT, AND NO-BODY LISTENS AND NOBODY COMES . . . "

Even Isabella is stunned.

"Evil little monsters, all of you." There is another of those awful hairball moments. As though Amos has just coughed up another gob of pain. "But now . . ."

Catching his breath, the old man gasps, "Welcome to Phase Two." Then he goes on in a perfectly reasonable tone. "In Phase Two, there will be a MegaMall in every part of the world. And in every MegaMall there will be a MegaTrail, so wherever you are hiding, you little wretches, watch out! I will catch you and I will teach you . . ."

Jule grabs Tick's arm.

The old man's voice fills the Great Room and echoes in all the galleries and corridors leading out to the far precincts of the Dark Hall. "And I won't rest until I've got you all!"

Now Amos stops unexpectedly. He raises a huge hand. Pointing to the corralled prisoners, he orders, "Take them away!"

Relieved, all of Zozzco Security rushes to obey. Prisoners fall into line obediently because wherever they are going is better than here. Anything is better than falling into the hands of vengeful, vicious Amos Zozz.

As they exit, the old man's voice fills the courtyard. "Wait!"

Security, prisoners, Zozzpeople and the two hiding on the onyx floor stop cold.

"First of all, thanks to the people who designed this, the first instrument in Phase Two. The talented . . ." A wet cough shakes Amos. His words blur.

To Tick they sound like . . . "Stileses."

Jule thinks she hears, "Devereaux family."

"Congratulations," Amos says in a voice that could split granite. "You folks made the cut. On to the staging platform, you will be airlifted shortly. Welcome to Phase Two."

Riveted, both the boy and the girl forget themselves. They scramble out from under the bench and lurch to their feet. They jump, trying to see over the heads of the crowd. Who does Amos have up there, waiting behind the velvet ropes, lined up to enter the next phase? They don't know. They have to see!

Jule murmurs, "Mom?"

The prisoners stand with their backs to the room and their hands tied behind them; there's no telling who they are.

Tick whispers, "Dad?"

"Now," Amos thunders, "take them away!"

Before Jule and Tick can identify the designers of the MegaTrail, before they can even see who they look like, Security turns them and marches them toward the exit.

"Oh, please," Jule murmurs, pushing through the crowd.

Tick's voice rattles urgently. "We have to hurry." He

tries to shoulder his way through the crowd but everybody is too distracted to hear. "I need you to move."

"Please." It's like pushing against a living wall. Jule is begging now, but it's too late. Before Jule and Tick can part the crowd— before they can take two steps toward the corridor where the captive designers are shuffling toward an unknown fate— the prisoners and their guards are gone.

TWENTY-FIVE

IT'S DARK IN HERE where they put him, and Doakie is soooo scared! Mommy says that when you say you're *soooo* something, you're supposed to say *that* something else. He is *sooooo* scared that . . . He can't think of the *that*.

First they got him in the cart and the cart went on down the tunnel and *down* the tunnel, he thought they were never going to stop. Once he saw Lance out the back but after that he didn't see Lance, he couldn't see anything except the awful people in the cart. He went in the tunnel because Puppy wasn't anywhere. Then they caught him and put him in the cart. At least Puppy got away, he thinks. He looked back when the cart drove off but he didn't see Puppy running and he didn't see him back there all mooshed on the tracks but it was dark, and you never know.

After they got him in the cart they rode and rode and rode.

The grownups talked and talked. One time Burt Arno got his mouth thing off and started yelling, so they wound tape around his whole head and that shut him up.

Finally the cart stopped at a place and everybody except

Doakie piled out, he couldn't because they had him tied up to the back rail. Up front Burt was fighting but they bopped him and put a bag over his head, then two big guys in black uniforms and big black bug helmets came and marched him away. First Doakie was scared they would take him too, and then for a long time it got so quiet in the tunnel that Doakie got scared that they wouldn't take him at all. Water dripped off the tunnel ceiling and some of it dripped on his head. All he could hear was this plop plop plop.

Then for a long time he didn't hear anything at all.

Then finally he heard people, two big guys and a really big lady, she was yelling at them to hurry, it was important. So something is very, very important, but Doakie doesn't know what. She said hurry or else and the guys were all weird and jerky getting on the cart, like they were only doing it because they were scared of the *or else*. Then she yelled while they undid the ropes and took Doakie off the cart. They wouldn't let him rub his wrists and they hurt *so much!*

He tried to ask who were they, but they didn't listen. He tried to ask was he going to jail, OK he's so hungry that he was thinking, *at least they would feed me in jail.*

Instead the big lady popped him into a great big box. Then they picked up the box and dumped it here.

Wherever *here* is.

It's dark in the box and Doakie doesn't know where he is. No Mom, it's _so_ dark in the box _that_ I don't know where I am. There. There's the _that_. He doesn't know where he is. He doesn't know where he is but that isn't the worst part, and he doesn't know what happened to Puppy but that isn't the worst part either.

The worst part is, he doesn't know what they're going to do to him.

Then all of a sudden the top pops off the box and a bunch of light comes in all at once, scaring Doakie, curled up here in the dark.

"It's time," somebody says. "Take him in."

TWENTY-SIX

NOW THAT YOU'VE SEEN my mighty rat trap," Amos says in a voice that overflows the room, "Bring in the rats!"

The crowd's *budda-budda-budda* turns into an ugly growl. "Rats."

Rats! Jule's heart crashes. The robed billionaire isn't just talking about Burt Arno. *Who else has he caught?*

Tick is craning to see. *How many?*

"Rats," Amos says triumphantly. "Rats to run in my mighty MegaTrail."

Who, they wonder. *Who?*

Now the crowd parts like the Red Sea and another squad in black uniforms with shiny black faceplates that make them look like bugs crashes through, leading a sullen little parade of kids that Jule and Tick know all too well.

The Crazies, every one of them.

The very people they were counting on to escape and bring help are now prisoners.

First Willie and James come in, handcuffed and silenced by duct tape. It's clear from the cuts and bruises on their faces that the boys fought hard before they were captured. Tick's two main men glower, but there's nothing they can do or say to change what's happened to them.

They are followed by the Crazies from the first wave of rafts to reach the underground dock.

Tick groans. *My people.*

Next comes Mag Sullivan, grimly clutching Puppy in her arms. Then Jiggy and Nance come in, followed by the smaller Crazies, knotted together by a long rope. Burt Arno's lieutenants Tidgewell, Bruno and Kirk come in, along with the battered remnants of the Dingo tribe, all tattered and grimy and struggling to free their hands.

Some of the night children are wet and limping after the battle in the grotto at the head of the Hidden River. It happened fast. Tick's forces fought hard against Amos's guards, but they were outnumbered. Now they are here.

Security has rounded up every single member of every crew in the little flotilla Tick Stiles brought to conquer the powers in the Dark Hall. As he and Jule watch, Security marches down the central aisle, herding all the boys and girls that Tick thought were safe on the fast-moving underground river, riding the rushing current out of the mall.

His last hope. Not a one escaped to carry the news to Castertown. Everyone he cares about is trapped.

The only friend Tick has left in the MegaMall is Lance, and he has no idea what's become of Lance. Then he thinks, *What can one big guy do against all this? What can any of us do?*

Give up, he supposes, but he won't.

This is the most important thing about Tick Stiles. He doesn't think about it, it's just part of who he is. This is what keeps him going. It's kept him going for years.

He never gives up.

As it turns out, neither does Jule. Her mind is whirring, whirring, looking for a plan. The rest comes so fast that neither could tell you which spoke first or who said what.

"It's up to us."

"We have to get out and get help."

They lock eyes. It is a little pledge. They need to escape, but this is not the time.

The sad parade is ending.

A bamboo cage rolls in, barely containing the gagged and furious Burt Arno. Like a caged gorilla, he keeps throwing himself against the bars. Fuming, Burt saws the ropes that bind his hands back and forth on one of the bars, trying to free himself.

A Zozzco vice president marks the tail of the procession. She is huge in a black uniform laden with gold stripes. She has a struggling child by the wrist. Holding him at arm's length so he can't kick her, she drags him along.

"Doakie!"

"That's everybody." Sadly, Tick shakes his head.

A drumroll sounds. Trumpet fanfare rings throughout the Great Room. In the stir that follows as the crowd closes behind the dismal parade, Jule and Tick struggle closer to the front of the mob. The Zozzpeople are far too upset and distracted to notice two interlopers.

The night children are beyond fear.

"At last." Amos Zozz pats his chest and laughs. His cackle is amplified in the Great Room. Every word resounds in all the galleries and corridors of the Dark Hall.

"My rats," he spits. "Children. Disgusting. Just like the idiot shoppers who made me rich."

Although Amos does not know it, his dry, harsh, angry voice doesn't stop here in the Great Room, and in spite of the seals and locks he put in place to keep goings-on in the Dark Hall secret, it doesn't stop at the forbidding doors to the Dark Hall, either. Every poisonous word of his rant is crackling in every part of the gigantic honeycomb that is the MegaMall.

"Children, running in my MegaTrail like rats, just like the shoppers that run in my MegaMall. Rodents, all of you," Amos bellows. "Do you know what you are? You're nothing but brainless, repulsive rats!"

Amos doesn't know it, but every word he says is being heard out there, in all the galleries and corridors, in every courtyard, food court and storefront in the Castertown MegaMall. His shocking words shake the entire mall.

Lance the Loner has done his job.

"Blind, greedy rats," Amos rants, "dancing to my tune! You shoppers come because your rat children beg you to come, and you shop. Buy, get, take, borrow so you can come back to buy some more, you are nothing more than mindless buying machines, and do you want to know why you spend yourself out of house and home?"

At a wave of his hand, the music starts. The tune is so familiar and so hateful that Tick bites his thumb.

"Because I want you to!

Spring and summer. Tick and Jule know the words.

"I feed on your greed!"

Winter, fall. They know them too well.

The music rises and Amos raises his voice to match it,

shouting, "BECAUSE I CAN MAKE YOU DO WHATEVER I WANT!"

At another wave of his hand, the music stops. There is a hush in the great room. The old man's wet whisper is louder than his shout. "With money comes power. And with power," he whispers, gloating, "comes control."

Spitefully, the old man sings, "Spring and summer, winter, fall. Cool kids shop at the MegaMall." The Zozzco jingle. Amos finishes with an ugly laugh. "Shop on, you stupid, greedy fools."

Would he be quiet if he knew everyone in the Mega-Mall could hear? Probably not. Driven by hatred, Amos is beyond it now.

"You're like rats, gnawing at goods in my wonderful MegaMall because I tell you to. Well, soon you rats will be flying to MegaMalls all over the world! And you will pay. You will pay plenty for the privilege, and," he adds with a sinister laugh, "As a special added attraction, I'll have *children* running like rats in all my MegaTrails, and *then* you'll see how powerful I am. Go ahead, spend yourselves into the poorhouse because you love shopping and you don't know how to stop." The laughter is getting wilder. "And I love to watch you beg and borrow and sell everything you have so you can shop some more because now I own you and I control you, you greedy, despicable rats."

Thanks to the complex connections and Bluetooth relays Lance put in place today before sunrise, the contempt of Amos Zozz reverberates in every nook, cranny, food court and gallery of the overbearing, pretentious structure he willed into being here.

"But first . . ."

Elsewhere in the MegaMall, the air changes. Something large is in motion. Lance the Loner has done his work indeed. He has done it well.

Amos points to Doakie: "Bring that child!"

Eager to get rid of Doakie, who kicks and bites, the uniformed woman yanks him along by the ear.

"Ow. Ow!"

At the sound of Doakie's yelp, Puppy squirms in Mag's arms, going, *hrr hrr hrr.* "Puppy, shh!" Mag closes her hand around the baby Scottie's muzzle to hush him up.

"Come on up here, little boy," Amos croons as Doakie stumbles forward. "Come on, miserable child. You can sit on my lap and watch them put the very first rats in my MegaTrail!" Amos tries to make it sound festive but he can't help himself; under his breath he adds, "Before I'm done, I'll trap every little rat in the world! Soon I'll have all my MegaTrails filled with you, and then . . ."

Thanks to Lance, the whisper inside the platinum helmet is magnified. Near and far, everyone in the MegaMall hears. Zozzpeople start their uneasy *buddabuddabudda*-ing.

Amos is so crazed that he is thinking out loud. His angry, frantic whisper rattles around and around inside the mask: "Then we drop in the hornets."

Jule and Tick exchange horrified looks.

Shivering, Doakie backs away.

Now Amos crooks his finger like the witch trying to lure Hansel and Gretel into his cottage so she can cook and eat them. "I won't hurt you, sonny," he says falsely. "Come on."

Doakie shakes his head.

"Come on, child, come sit with me," Amos says in the sticky voice that only stupid adults use with little kids. "Or else."

"No!"

But Amos Zozz, billionaire builder and global entrepreneur isn't used to waiting. "Coooome on . . . Come on, you little . . . OK then!" Irritated, he shouts, "Guards, grab him!"

Doakie breaks and runs, but two burly Security guards pull him down in mid-flight.

With a little cry, Jule lunges to save him.

Tick grabs her arm. *"What are you doing?"*

"Let go!"

The glassy MegaTrail is so huge, the captive night children are so young and the suspense is so awful that the Zozzpeople standing nearby don't see or hear the two arguing in tones so low that they might be listening to each other think.

"We have to help!"

"We can't get caught."

"We can't let this happen!"

"We won't." Grimly, Tick says, *"We have to get out and tell the world."*

Jule doesn't argue. She is learning. She doesn't stop to ask questions. She does as she is told.

Now Security is passing Doakie over the heads of the crowd like a little log. Now they are handing him up to the dais where the stark chair stands. Now the black-robed billionaire in the tall boots and the cruelly handsome platinum mask sits on his throne and takes Doakie on his bony lap.

Now that he has Doakie, Amos croons in a voice so bland that it is positively creepy. "What a lovely little boy." Then his voice turns hard and loud.

"I had a little boy once." Amos is talking to Doakie, but he is looking at Isabella.

The tall, vain and ambitious daughter of Amos Zozz rocks as though he just slapped her face. He is really talking to her.

"Rather, my daughter Isabella had a little boy, but he was an UNGRATEFUL LITTLE BRUTE."

Nailed by a spotlight, Isabella flinches.

Outside the Great Room, beyond the six entrances to the Dark Hall, something is changing, although Amos doesn't know it yet.

On the old man's lap, Doakie is bawling. Puppy hears him crying and like greased sunshine, squirms out of Mag's arms and with a leap, escapes from the crowd, skibbling over the onyx with his little claws tapping as he runs to rescue Doakie Jinks.

The old man's voice shakes the room. "WE HAD OUR OWN LITTLE BOY, BUT HE DIDN'T LIKE WHAT WE ARE DOING HERE." Such a big voice, here in the Dark Hall.

Elsewhere in the MegaMall, out of sight and out of hearing, there is an ominous stir.

"MY SPIT AND IMAGE, BUT HE WAS ORNERY."

Jule locks hands with Tick. *Yes. Tell the world.*

On the old man's lap, Doakie sobs and sobs. Poor Doak, he can't help blubbering, he's that scared.

"SO WE SENT HIM AWAY."

Such a big voice, going out through amplifiers all over the Castertown MegaMall.

"Too bad, now that I have just the place for him he's vanished. But you'll do nicely." Amos pats Doakie on the head. "My little rat. Now, for years I have run this place with one thing in mind, and you bring your stupid mommies and daddies out here by the carload and you eat what I tell you and buy what I say. You gawk at the things I build to deceive you, and then you eat some more and drink what I provide, so you'll go running out to buy more, and what do you think you are?"

It's impossible for the old man's bitter rant to get any louder, but it does. "You are all my rats. Buy. Take. Get, get, get, greedy, mindless scum of the earth." Gripping Doakie by the collar, he swivels, pointing to his squadrons of Security and quivering Zozzpeople. "Any questions?"

Nobody speaks. They're all too scared.

"Well," he shouts to all assembled, "WHETHER OR NOT YOU ASK QUESTIONS, I HAVE ANSWERS."

Caught up in the moment, the old man trumpets to the skies: "IT'S ANSWER TIME."

Bent on revenge as he is, Amos barely feels it when Doakie sinks sharp teeth into the web of his bony right hand. Absently, he bats the boy's cheek. "Stop that."

Like that! Puppy comes bounding up on the platform. Doakie cries, "Puppy!"

"Hush!" Amos pulls back his hand to hit Doakie again.

Growling, brave little Puppy sinks his teeth into the old man's bare white shin just above the shiny gold boot.

"Ow!" Amos kicks the baby dog so hard that he flies off the dais.

Puppy goes flying into the crowd crying, "Yip-yip-yip."

"You made me rich . . ."

Amos goes on talking as though his leg doesn't hurt and there is no blood dripping down inside his beautiful boot. "But you might as well know . . ."

A gob of spit rattles in the old man's throat. He hocks it up and out on the platform and talks on, so wrapped up in what he's saying that he barely notices when he loses his grip on his little prisoner and Doakie slips away.

"I despise you all!

"I despise your mindless greed and I'm sick of watching you shop in my MegaMall, I'm tired of watching you get naked in the dressing rooms, preening in front of my hidden cameras and I hate seeing all the sordid, secret things you do in obscure corners in my magnificent Mega-Mall, and you want to know why?"

No one dares answer.

"Well, do you?"

In the thunderous silence that follows, everybody in the Great Room and thousands of shoppers, store clerks, security and support personnel in every far-flung sector of the MegaMall look up in horror.

"Do you want to know why I despise you?"

Where ads had been playing on giant plasma screens in every sector when all this began, the screens through-out the MegaMall show only one picture now. The image of Amos Zozz is magnified a hundredfold on every screen. The platinum mask glistens like a diamond-studded skull.

"Well, I'll tell you why."

Howling with fury, Amos rips off the glittering mask. "LOOK WHAT YOU DID TO ME!"

How could they not? The ghastly image fills every screen.

The image on a thousand giant screens is much, much more terrible because without the mask, the naked head of Amos Zozz isn't really naked.

It only looks undressed because he has removed the mask. Yes, it's red and raw and completely hairless. There are no eyebrows on this evil face, no eyelashes. Indeed, there's not a single hair. Pale white skin covers the top of his skull, but the head of Amos Zozz is by no means naked.

There are dozens upon dozens of oversized, disfiguring lumps all over Amos Zozz's face and scalp, hideous lumps that stand out on his neck and his ears and even bigger lumps that rise like anthills on that great big, revoltingly hairless head. Amos seems not to care. He flashes square yellow teeth in a smile of pure hatred.

By this time the people of the MegaMall are on the move. Outraged, they rush past the video screens, funneling into the galleries and corridors to join the mob. The mob flows as swiftly as the underground river, but this is different. These are living people with real feelings, and what they feel right now, in spite of the tranquilizers Amos has piped into their water over the years, is rage.

They are heading for the Dark Hall.

Hypnotized by his own rhetoric, Amos has no idea.

Fixed on the little show on the dais, nobody in the Great Room knows what is coming. The people of the Mega-Mall are marching on the enemy, and they are coming in such great numbers that there will be no stopping them.

And Amos rages on. "I took your money and you

thanked me. I made you dance to my tune, and now . . . ," he says triumphantly, "you will all do my bidding, and YOU CHILDREN WILL SUFFER FOR WHAT YOU DID TO ME!" Powerful Amos Zozz is blazing mad. "NOW, WHERE IS THAT BOY?"

As he whirls in his black cape, preparing to issue the next order, everything changes. Everybody but Amos is too frightened and distracted to know.

"Catch that child!" Amos shouts at top volume. "Throw him in the MegaTrail! Soon all you children will be running in my MegaTrail, and you, my despicable shoppers, will pay extra just to watch me . . ." Bloated with fury, Amos looms.

"JUST TO WATCH ME POUR IN THE HORNETS AND LISTEN TO ME LAUGH!"

My people. A shudder runs through Tick like a bad wind. Smart and cautious as he is, he can't let this happen. *I have to take care of them!*

Amos shouts, "Security! Put the captives in the Mega-Trail!"

"No." Gallant, foolhardy Tick Stiles jumps up on a bench and raises his fist, shouting over the din, "No!"

Jule jumps up to stand there beside Tick. "We can stop him!" she shouts to the crowd. "He's only one person."

"Not so fast!" Like a great dictator, Amos stamps on a raised brass button in the floor. Elsewhere, an alarm will sound. In the world according to Amos, this should bring out the Dark Hall emergency squad, but nothing changes. Meanwhile, the vibration in the floor has turned into a drum-drumming, but the people in the Great Room are too distressed to notice. For a second, everyone is still.

Now that he has their attention, Tick shouts, "Please. Help us."

"Come on, everybody," Jule cries. "We need you all." And independent, opinionated Jule Devereaux, who thought she could handle everything by herself, Jule is pleading with the people in the Dark Hall, "We can't do this without you!"

Amos shouts, "Grab those children!"

Meanwhile the Zozzpeople look at each other, questioning. Join them? Turn on Amos? Stay with Amos? They don't know. Looking at them, the night children have no idea which way it will go.

"Get them!"

TWENTY-SEVEN

THE DRUMMING OF MARCHING feet grows as people march on the Dark Hall by the thousands. Nobody in the Great Room hears what is coming. The Zozzpeople don't notice the vibration; Security doesn't. They are all fixed on the crisis. What are they going to do?

Should they do as Amos orders?

Should they help Tick and Jule? Will they? What will happen to the night children if they don't?

What will happen to them if they do?

"Shall we?" "Would we?" "Should we?" The Zozz-people can't seem to agree.

Then they do.

First it's no more than one person muttering, "But we'll lose our promotions!" The corporate *buddabuddabudda* turns hostile. "We want our promotions." A shout rises. "We can't lose the money." "What about our raises?" "We want our raises." The protest grows. "We want the stripes!"

"Survival," someone yells.

There is a loud group cry. "Yeeeaaah."

"Survival of the fittest!"

Everyone yells louder, "Yaaaaay."

Just when things seem to be going the old man's way, some brave person says, "But they're only *children*. We can't just . . ."

Isabella's shout cuts through this like a knife. "Stop!"

All heads turn.

"Think about it." Coldly, she asks, "What's this really about?"

Massed Zozzpeople whisper as one: "We're afraid of him."

"Exactly. And with good reason." Isabella says in that icy voice, "Now, do as my father says."

"All right then." The old man points that terrible, long finger. "Get them!"

The tension breaks. Everybody lunges at once. Hands close on Jule and Tick. "Gotcha!"

"At last." Amos Zozz raises his fist. "All hail the corporation."

His obedient creatures recite in unison, "All hail the corporation."

"Glory to Zozzco."

"Glory to Zozzco!"

Like a grotesque cheerleader, the tycoon trumpets, "On to Phase Two."

Nervously, the Zozzpeople parrot, "On to Phase Two."

Amos pushes a button in the side of the tall chair. Elsewhere, multiple engines start up, but the crowd is too distracted to know.

"Now bring me those two! You, treacherous girl!" Raging, Amos points at Jule. He turns his glare on Tick.

"And you, pernicious boy. You are my rats." He thunders, "PUT THEM IN MY MEGATRAIL."

Impatient because his Zozzpeople aren't moving fast enough, the old man comes down off the platform and makes a grab first for Jule, then for Tick.

At that exact moment, everything— the air, the stone underfoot— seems to shift.

Somewhere far from the Great Room, doors crash wide. The Dark Hall is no longer sealed.

Something big is approaching. Everybody knows it now. The vibration in the onyx floor becomes a little earthquake as whatever is coming— and it sounds like legions upon legions tramping— approaches.

As it turns out, the first wave is closer than you think.

Unlike the angry mall employees and the legions of outraged shoppers, the first to arrive are the real citizens of the MegaMall. They reach the Great Room through a secret entrance only the Zozz family knows about.

Led by a familiar figure in camo and a ski mask, the night children come pouring in.

The lost tribes march in front— people Tick has never seen in all his years of living here, people that his Crazies and the Dingos would never encounter in ordinary times, people Jule Devereaux never knew about, and she has come here almost every day of her life. On they come, hundreds of boys and girls from unknown tribes in dozens of shopping sectors where only Lance has traveled.

The little army includes children so timid that they never go out and children who are afraid of adults and ones who are so shy that they seldom speak, but all of them are here today because Lance the Loner sent out the call and before anything, the night children are loyal.

The Loner's prerecorded sound bite alerted all the tribes of children well before the MegaMall opened for business. The summons was heard in every sector exactly as Lance intended. He set the timer when he programmed the system back in the Communications Center well before dawn.

His announcement named the many routes to the secret Zozz family corridor. It set the time.

As soon as they heard the call, the tribes dropped whatever they were doing and hit the ground running. They hopped on trams or commandeered bicycles from sporting goods stores or grabbed the mall's motorized wheelchairs, anything to be here, where they are needed.

When they are alone, most children aren't particularly frightening.

Marching together like this, for a good cause, they are magnificent. Excited. Powerful. Ready to serve. There are so many that even Lance the Loner doesn't know them all. There are more of them in the corridor and more children flooding into the Great Room, marching shoulder to shoulder, than anyone could imagine.

Meanwhile, the adults march on, toward the master of the Dark Hall. Alerted by the voice of Amos, blasting into corridors live and in full cry by the time the MegaMall opened for business, shoppers and staff in great numbers come streaming through the galleries of the Dark Hall, heading for the Great Room.

Everything is changing.

Amos knows it now.

Now, Amos Zozz, the vengeful spirit of the Dark Hall and creator of the MegaMall, may be barking mad, but he is by no means stupid. Standing like a statue about to be toppled, he taps a device hanging from his belt. Far from the scene, hidden forces register the command. Engines roar as his steel birds take the air.

Mystified, Jule and Tick watch the old tyrant.

At the center of the dais, Amos pauses. He tilts his head. He is *listening.*

The massed children and Zozzpeople here in the heart of the Dark Hall are much too caught up in what's going on to hear what Amos is listening for: the WHAP WHAP WHAP of beating propellers. With a nod he looks up, into the center of the smoked dome overhead, as though checking for something.

The crowd is too angry and disrupted to look up and see what Amos sees— moving shadows above the smoked glass of the dome, the movement of great whirling blades silhouetted against blazing sunlight.

Reassured, the arrogant old man rakes the room with his eyes. As the night children advance on the dais, he shouts into a microspeaker that magnifies his voice.

It fills the Dark Hall. "Stop them!"

Even Amos should see that it's too late.

On the night children come, advancing in such numbers that the minions of Amos Zozz are overwhelmed before they can fight back— that is, if they wanted to fight back. The way things are right now, this is by no means certain. The witless vice presidents in their gaudy uniforms and the squads of armed Security don't know what they want, except for this to be over.

The young invaders cut through the confused Zozz-people and the flock of milling guards like a flying arrow.

Tall in the camo and the heavy boots, forbidding in the ski mask, Lance the Loner is walking point. As the crowd parts, Lance jumps up on the platform to confront Amos Zozz, a voice they all know rises in a loud, clear shriek. "Son!"

It is Isabella Zozz.

Everyone in the Great Room falls silent.

The old man turns on Lance, thunderstruck. "You."

Tick grips Jule's hand. They have stopped breathing.

Finally Lance speaks, louder than he's spoken in years, "Yeah Grampa, it's me."

"How could you?"

Everyone's breath comes out at once. *"Grampa!"*

Lance turns to them with an embarrassed shrug. "Sorry about that."

Leaping to the dais, towering over Amos Zozz in his faded camouflage, Lance the Loner pulls off the ski mask. His young face is like a mask even when it isn't covered— handsome but neutral. White-blond hair. To the end, Lance is careful not to let people know what he is feeling. "Old man, it's over."

Next to Amos, his vain daughter Isabella wails, "Oh Lance, how could you!"

"Sorry, Mom," Lance says to Isabella Zozz. "I tried to warn you, but you wouldn't listen."

The night children gasp. *Mom!*

Lance clamps his hands on the old man's shoulders. "I tried to make you stop. And you wouldn't listen."

Shaking him off, Amos bellows like an enraged bull. "You're just a kid."

"What you're doing here is wrong."

With a flip of his black cape, Amos stalks to the ebony chair planted on the dais.

The loner turns to Isabella. "It's over."

"But Lance," she cries. "It's what I do for a living!"

Lance the Loner says harshly, "Not any more."

Outside the Dark Hall, there is a *boom*. It is the slow, relentless thud of something heavy hitting the tall double doors that seal the Great Room.

"Noooo," Isabella cries. "My son, my future!"

Boom.

"Mother, it's got to stop."

"Children!" Amos snorts. "Children. How can you stop me with a bunch of children?" At the same time he pushes a second button embedded in the back of the ebony chair. Somewhere inside the walls of the Great Room, machinery begins to whir. Too slowly for anyone to notice, the chair begins to rise.

There is another *Boom*. This one is louder.

Lance says coldly, "Do you hear that?"

"I DON'T HEAR ANYTHING." Jumping up on the chair, the once-imperious Amos forgets himself. Confused by the racket, he yells at Lance like a cranky grandfather, which is what he is, "Go to your room!"

Boom.

Lance throws back his head and for the first time since he and Tick Stiles met ten years ago, Tick hears him laugh.

The night children are only the front ranks of what's coming.

Boom.

What follows is too big even for Amos Zozz.

Before the MegaMall's founder and owner can rally his milling Zozzpeople or unleash Security, the adult world comes down on Amos Zozz.

Boom. The giant double doors to the Great Room fly open with a smash and the outside world comes in.

But remember, Amos is standing on that chair.

Suddenly the light in the Great Room changes.

Above, a pie-shaped wedge appears in the smoked glass dome. Jule, Tick, everybody in the courtyard will be too wild and distracted to see the first sliver of sunlight streaming in as the dome opens and the air fills with the sound of whirring metal blades.

They are fixed on the downfall of Amos Zozz. It's all they can think about right now. It's all they see.

Fueled by outrage, the people of Castertown and shoppers from every state and nation come pouring in. Now adults flood the Great Room in such great numbers that it's hard to make out their faces.

Brandishing brooms and squeegees, the cleaning crews come first and, armed with tools of every description, the maintenance people come. Then come shoppers by the hundreds to be followed by thousands more, alerted by the ranting of Amos Zozz when they entered the MegaMall, thanks to the mallwide communications system masterminded by Lance the Loner in the quiet early hours before he locked the door on the Communications Center and led the attack on the Dark Hall.

As the adults march in, bearing weapons, Jule and Tick back away. Working together, they free the Crazies and the Dingos; Tick opens the cage and unties Burt, who claps him on the back in a grudging thank-you. The night children back away from the scene, all but Lance, who watches his friends and allies go with an expression no one here will be able to decipher.

Like it or not, Lance the Loner is in command now.

More alone than ever.

Lance has had enough. "Get down, Gramps," he says to the old man standing on the tall ebony chair. "It's over now."

"No," Amos screams. "Stand down!"

And Lance the Loner responds in a voice full of thunder, "Never!"

"Wait, son." Amos cries in a desperate stab at saving the situation, "All this could be yours!"

"Well, I don't want it!"

"All right for you!" The billionaire's arm comes down like the axe at a beheading. It is a signal.

Lines drop through the dome, snaking around Amos. Uniformed men slide down heavy ropes: the Zozzco helicopter rescue squad. As they scoop him up Amos wails, "Why, Lance?"

Lance never talked much. He doesn't speak now.

The defeated billionaire cries, "Why?"

Watching as Amos puts his foot in the loop of a snaking rope and rises to the skies, Lance the Loner, who has finally come into his own, says in a voice that carries up into the dome and out along the long galleries, resounding throughout the MegaMall:

"Because you can't treat people that way."

EPILOGUE

IT WILL BE DAYS before the Castertown MegaMall sorts itself out after the revolution. It will probably be weeks or months before business goes back to normal, if there is a normal in the biggest shopping center in the entire world.

The first thing Lance did after the fall was to destroy the supply of tranquilizers Amos had technicians dumping into the river daily. Heads in Castertown are clearer now, although only Lance knows why. For the first time since Amos Zozz came to the prairie with his master plan and his Zozzco jingle, people are thinking for themselves.

In a shopping world liberated by children, adults are taking charge. The night children— Lance, Tick, the others— prefer it that way. Their time will come, just not yet. Right now they're enjoying being who they are.

By the time the adults present— store clerks, managers, the few Zozzco vice presidents hired by the mayor of Castertown to take over the MegaMall management— finish the dozens of conferences and meetings it will take to get the place organized and running properly . . .

By the time the adults in charge decide to go looking

for the night children, Tick's Castertown Crazies and the Dingos and all the other tribes that haunt the mall will have completely vanished from the scene, because before they know anything, the night children know how to disappear.

In fact, by the time Amos Zozz left the building the way he did, most of the night children were already on their way out of the Great Room, down corridors leading away from the Dark Hall. One by one they slipped back into the fabric of the mall.

Of course the tribes are much smaller now.

Some of the night children have been reunited with their families.

They found mothers or fathers in the throng on the day of the downfall. Some parents found children they had given up for lost, and the reunions were sweet.

In the confusing weeks that followed the overthrow of Amos Zozz, there were more reunions. Some children searched for their parents among the old man's discarded prisoners and found them— rejected designers and builders and unwanted workers, freed after years of slavery in the Dark Hall.

Some parents used the Communications Center to reach children they had given up for lost. Then there are the old man's "chosen" prisoners. The few who were picked to follow up in Phase Two aren't anywhere, and some of them have children living here. After a futile search, their children have gone back to their tribes.

Naturally, the orphans among the night children are perfectly happy where they are, living in the nooks and crannies of this commercial paradise. Some are just happy to be living far from evil guardians.

Others quite simply love the life and, frankly, don't want to be found.

Don't feel sorry for them. Children without parents can always find a way to survive.

They're here to tell you that if you don't let loneliness hurt you, it will make you strong. Losing someone you love makes you think. It makes you resourceful.

Put to the test, children who have lost a parent do what they have to, and they do it as well as they possibly can. With others like them, they have settled back into their lives in the Castertown MegaMall.

Now the tribes are all safely hidden in their various deserted shops and vacant storage areas, where they have set up housekeeping because right now, this looks like the best place. They'll stay where they are until somebody stumbles onto them and it's time to move again.

In fact, the true night children love their hideouts and they love the game, the running and the hiding in places where no grownups come. They love the freedom, the nights of playing in the courtyards and galleries of the complex when the daytime world goes home and goes to sleep.

They love the MegaMall, where they'll go on living for as long as they want to before they outgrow this place and decide to leave it because it's time to grow up in the world.

For Jule and Tick, however, the long night and the days to follow have raised questions. Before Amos left, he sent his chosen architects and designers off to a loading zone to be shipped out to open Phase Two.

They haven't been seen since.

Are their parents among them? They don't know. When the chosen were marched away, the boy and the girl were flat on their bellies on the onyx, lying low. They were lying so low that they never saw any faces. Some days they think their parents were in the Great Room that morning. Other days, they just don't know.

They have been talking about it ever since.

Jule says, "That was them up there on the platform, wasn't it? My mom and dad? Yours?"

Not for the first time, Tick says, "I don't know."

"Well, what do you think?"

"Yes. I think so," he says, frustrated. Then he says, "No. I don't know."

"I wish I could tell you," Lance says to them, "but I don't know."

The three of them are sitting on the loading dock underneath the abandoned music store, swinging their feet. Lance still sits tall in his camouflage, but the ski mask is gone and his white-blond hair stands up in bright spikes.

"All I can tell you is," Lance says, "they aren't in the Dark Hall." His voice drops. "At least not any more."

Not for the first time Jule says, "If we knew where he took them, we could go there and look for them."

"*If* he took them," Tick says pointedly.

"I wish I could tell you what he did." Lance grimaces. "Thing is, we've scoured this place. If your folks were still in the mall, I'd know."

Tick throws a penny at the tracks below and listens as it hits with a clink. "We've been everywhere and there's no sign."

Stubbornly, Jule says, "But we don't know for sure that

they're gone." They've been over this so many times that even Jule is tired.

Tick draws up his feet, hugging his knees. "Maybe the police."

Jule turns to Lance. "We could ask your mom, but we don't know where she is."

He shrugs. "The minute it came down she was out of here."

"Maybe she's in hiding."

"No. My guess is, she's wherever the helicopters took Grampa."

"That was awesome!" Tick grins in spite of himself. "Who knew the dome would open up like that? Who knew that chair of his was an elevator thing? Who do you think took him?"

Jule tries, "I wanted a SWAT team, or the FBI."

"Helicopters, remember?" Lance, who never lets anyone know what he's thinking, is openly frustrated. "Zozzco helicopters. They'll never catch him now. He's gone to . . . I don't know. My guess is, a secret base. He has hideouts nobody knows about."

Tick bares his teeth. "There are a lot of things nobody knows."

But Jule can't give up. "The prisoners too? What about the prisoners?"

Lance says gently, "You might as well know, Grampa's got bunkers and castles and desert fortresses all over the place. China, Canada. He could have them locked up anywhere in the world."

"All this," Jule says. "All that trouble and we still don't know. It's crazy, facing Amos and still not knowing."

Tick moves his hand on the dock so that their fingers are touching. "Books end," he tells her. "Life goes on."

There is a long silence.

To make them both feel better, Jule says, "At least Doakie found his mom."

"Or she found him." Tick is grinning. "And she *apologized*. That was pretty cool."

"He was pretty glad to see her."

"Yeah, but he was crying when he left."

"It's OK," Tick says. "He has Puppy to take care of him."

"I'll miss him." Jule makes a business of not feeling sorry for herself, but she can't keep from saying, "We should all be so lucky."

"But we're not." To make her feel better, Tick says, "At least this place is back to normal."

It's amazing. Lance laughs! "As normal as it gets."

Jule turns to him. "You're going to run it now, right? The MegaMall? Now that they're gone?"

"No. No way."

"But you're the . . ."

"Best? Forget it. No way." Lance goes on, "Not on your life. I put some good people in control."

"By all rights the place is yours."

Lance shakes his head. "It's not anything I want, OK? It's nothing I ever wanted, which is why I got on their case." He grins. "The Castertown City Council can take care of it now that they're back in their right minds."

Tick says, "You mean the water."

"Amazing what tranquilizers will do." Lance gets up. "Let them handle it. I'm done."

"But you could . . ."

"No. Don't worry. It's OK. There won't be any more . . . Any more . . ." They are all thinking about the living displays, the captive architects and designers, the spycams in every dressing room. The MegaTrail! "Any more . . ." Lance spreads his hands but there aren't enough words to fill them. "Whatever that was he did! At least, not here."

"What are you going to . . ." By the time Jule finishes the question, Lance is gone. ". . . do? Wow, that was fast! Where did he . . ."

"Go? Back to his place, I guess."

"Weird," she says. "He could own all this, but he'd rather live down here, with us."

"Beholden to no one." Tick shrugs. "If he has to, Lance will take over, but not right away. He has what he wants. For now."

She gives him a sharp look. "What about you? Do you have what you want?"

The boy considers for a long minute. He seems to be studying the empty tunnel, the endless stretch of empty track. He says in a low voice, "I like knowing where I am."

"Don't you want to know where *they* are?"

"I do." Tick's voice drops to a serious place. "But there's nothing I can do about it until I find out what's going on."

"If those were our parents," Jule says, just the way she does every time, "we need to find our parents. Or I do. I have to go look for them. You?"

The smile Tick turns to her is sweet and complicated and makes clear that there's no point arguing.

"The Crazies," he says, and that's all he needs to say.

His people. Depending on him. There is no leaving until they are all grown and he knows they're going to be fine.

Still she tries, "I just thought maybe if there were two of us . . . No use asking you to come look for them, is there?"

"I have things to do and people to take care of." He gives her that smile. "You're welcome to stay."

"I can't go home," Jule says, but she has come a long way since the day she ignored that LAST CALL. "I know I can't find Mom and Dad and Aunt Christy without help, but that doesn't mean I want to spend the rest of my life going around on the WhirlyFunRide, either. See what I mean?"

"I do."

"So I don't know what to do."

Standing, Tick holds out his hand. "Tell you what."

She takes it and lets him help her up. They are standing eye to eye now, Tick a little taller, Jule rising slightly on her toes. When she asks, she is asking more than an immediate question. "What?"

She is waiting.

So is he.

When he doesn't answer, she says again, "What?"

Then Tick's face breaks into a great big Castertown Crazy grin and he says, "Why don't you stay here with us until you figure it out?"

Kit Reed is the author of the Alex Award–winning *Thinner Than Thou* and many other novels. Reed has been nominated for the World Fantasy Award, and collections of her short fiction have been finalists for the James Tiptree, Jr., Award. Kit Reed lives in Middletown, Connecticut, where she is Resident Writer at Wesleyan University. *The Night Children* is her first book for young readers.